I don't want to sing

Meg Glyn

I don't want to sing

Copyright © 2001 Meg Glyn

Reprinted 2004

ISBN 1 903607 15 9

All rights reserved. No part of this publication may be reproduced, stored in a retrieval system or transmitted in any form or by any means electronic, mechanical, photocopying or otherwise without the prior permission in writing of the author.

typesetting and production by:

Able Publishing
13 Station Road, Knebworth, Herts SG3 6AP
Tel: 01438 812320 / 814316 Fax: 01438 815232
email: books@ablepublishing.co.uk
web site: www.ablepublishing.co.uk

I dedicate this book to the memory of my grandson, Carl, who was tragically taken from us aged eighteen years.

I wish to thank Jayne for all her help, Pauline who encouraged me to write on and, of course, my two children, Patricia and Eamonn.

Rehema

I do hope you enjoy my life story & not find it too Vulgar. etc.
It's nice having a chat with you.
Thank you for your help in 2006 + all the Best to you for 2007
   Best Wishes. God Bless,
         Meg Glynn.

Should you need any more Book for Presents e/c. Please Ring me on 217683.
   Books Price £5.99 But not for Yours

             Jan 2007

CHAPTER ONE

"Come on now, let's sing," Helen would say to the children, especially when they were hungry. She herself loved singing so much that she had convinced herself that singing could make her, and her two younger brothers and little sister, forget about the hunger.

"Come on now," she would say, "What shall it be, 'Danny Boy'?" Helen would pretend she was conducting a choir, but she would always allow James or Megan to choose what they would sing. It was more often James who would get what he wanted, otherwise he would beat hell out of Megan who was only three, and the youngest of the four children. Helen herself, only thirteen but much older than her years, had been left to care for herself and the three younger children after both parents died within a year of each other.

She was doing so on an income of 10 shillings per week – the Orphans Pension of 2/6 for each child. Their older brother, Leonard, who was sixteen years old, worked on a farm about six miles out of town, where he also earned 10 shillings for a six-day week.

He gave the money to Helen, which made £1 to keep the four of them, though Leonard also got a good meal each day from the farmer's wife; the only meal he had all day. He was also sometimes able to bring a few eggs home, or maybe a few turfs of peat tied in a sling to his old bike.

Their mother had been a seamstress, and even though she had suffered badly from arthritis, she had always contrived to keep food on the table. As well as sewing for the poor of the town, she would make patchwork quilts from any bits of material she could salvage. Her husband, the children's father, who was an odd-job man, would take the quilts out on his rounds, and sell them for five shillings each – in theory. He always hoped to get five shillings for a quilt, but sometimes people didn't have the money, so instead they would give him a load of turf, or ornaments, or some old items of clothing, which his wife would either cut down for the children or repair and sell on.

When she died things got really bad. Their poor father became so desperate with the worry that he himself died exactly one year to the day later. His wife had died on the 23 February one year, and he went to join her on 23 February the next year.

Helen and Leonard had promised their father on his deathbed, that they would never let the younger children be put in the workhouse if they could prevent it. Helen used to say that if their father had died and left mother, things would have been different – their mother being the stronger character. However, it wasn't to be, so Helen and Leonard were left to cope as best they could.

For a short while they managed, partly by selling items from their little home. An old Jew man (as people called them in those days) would come down from Dublin every few weeks, knocking on doors, asking people if they had anything to sell. He would force down the price if he could see they needed the money very badly, until he got them for next to nothing. This he did to poor Helen, until there was hardly anything left on the lovely dresser, which her mother had been so very proud of. The dresser had been filled with a variety of ornaments, mainly collected by their father in return for quilts. Now there wasn't much left worth selling, apart from a set of jugs which their Grandfather had given their mother when she had got married. The old Jew man would call now and again to see if Helen had changed her mind about the jugs, for he could see things were getting worse by the day. Peter, who had always been delicate, was getting skinnier; James, who was a bully was getting more bad-tempered, and was beating everyone up, and poor Megan, who had always loved singing with Helen, now refused to sing, saying, "I don't want to sing, I'm hungry, singing doesn't take my hunger away any more."

It was hearing Megan say that which made Helen go looking for the old Jew man. He was like Fagin, as Helen handed over the jugs for a pound. "No more," the Jew man said, "take it or leave it."

Of course she had to take the pound note. We have to have food, Helen thought. She expected Leonard to go mad when he saw the jugs gone, but he was reasonable about it, though he was very annoyed when he heard how little the Jew man had given her for them. The money soon went, and after that things were even worse.

Leonard came home one night to find the place in darkness. "God!" he said. No paraffin for the lamp, nor was there any smoke coming out of the chimney, which meant no turf. As he came into the house he could hear Megan whimpering, so he took the lamp from his bike, and running to where Helen and Megan slept found Helen in bed, and Megan lying beside her crying. As he shone the light on Helen he could see that she was very sick, and although the house was freezing cold, the sweat was pouring off her. He ran next door to get Mrs Murray, who also had a large family.

"Run, run!" Mrs Murray exclaimed as soon as she saw Helen, "Run down and get the doctor from town."

"But I haven't any money," Leonard said.

"Never mind about that," Mrs Murray said, "just tell him to come quick. I'll tell him when he gets here. Run now, be quick!"

Mrs Murray knew what would happen when the doctor came. He would see the conditions the children were living in, no fire, no food, no light. Mrs Murray tried to talk to the doctor, telling him about their parents, but she couldn't hold back the tears and ran back to get her husband, and to bring a lamp.

No sooner had Mr Murray returned with the lamp, than he heard the doctor tell Leonard that Helen had rheumatic fever, and that someone would be coming to take her away to the hospital. Mr Murray followed the doctor to show him out with the lamp, and took the opportunity to tell him about their father making Helen and Leonard promise not to let the children be put away.

"Well," the doctor said, "I have to report what I see. Then it is up to the authorities what they do."

Within a few hours Helen and the children were gone, pulled

out in the middle of the night, Helen in hospital, the three children in a workhouse operated by the Sisters of Mercy.

When the children arrived at the home, one of the nuns who staffed it bent down to pick Megan up. As she did so, her heavy pectoral crucifix hit Megan in the face, making her cry. That set off James, who up to then had not been crying though he had looked terrified. As for poor Peter, he looked too sick to care either way.

As the big door banged behind them the nun chivvied them along, demanding that 'they stop that crying, lest they wake the babies.' At the end of the corridor they were shown into a room full of rows of iron cots, most with babies in them, some crying, and being tended by a few girls. Pointing to a bench, the nun said, "Now you wait here and I'll go and get some cocoa and bread."

Hearing that, Megan said between tears, "Peter doesn't like cocoa, he only likes tea."

"He'll take what I give him," the nun said, closing the door behind her.

When the nun returned with the food, she said, "Right, while you're eating this I'll go and see where you're all going to sleep." The three children all ate the bread, and James and Megan drank their cocoa, including Peter's.

Again the door flew open. This time it was a young girl carrying a basket. "What's your name, dear?" she asked.

"Megan," Peter answered for her, looking very worried about what was going to happen to her. Peter had always been a very quiet child and very protective of Megan.

Looking at Peter's big, troubled, brown eyes the girl said, "Don't worry yourself, she'll be alright, you'll see her in the morning."

She led Megan along the same corridor, with its high ceiling, whitewashed walls and stone floors. Then she opened a door, and when Megan saw what was inside, she pulled back. "I want Helen, I want Helen!" she cried. The girl paid her cries no heed, but lifted her up and carried her to where she would sleep. Megan looked around, petrified, at these shaven-headed things in striped shirts. You couldn't tell if they were men or women.

As the girl clothed Megan in a similar striped night-shirt, she asked, "Do you want to do a wee?"

Megan nodded no, not knowing whether she did or she didn't want to do a wee. As the young girl closed the door behind her, Megan could hear the key turning in the lock. She did go to sleep, but was woken many times during the night by the sound of one of those white-haired creatures trying the door, muttering to themselves, moaning.

Next morning Megan got out of bed and, dragging the long, wet striped shirt, made her way to the door, only to find it still locked. She screamed and screamed, the fear having rooted her to the spot, as one of those creatures made its way towards her.

"Oh, you naughty child!" the nun said as she opened the door, "You'll upset everyone with your screaming, now stop it immediately!"

"Take her and wash her," she said to a young girl who had come with her.

"Where are your clothes?" the girl asked Megan.

"I don't know," she replied, "they might be down there," she added pointing to where she had slept.

"You sit here, I'll go and have a look," the girl told Megan.

At breakfast, the children noticed that apart from the young girls and the babies, there were no other children but themselves anywhere to be seen.

After she had been scrubbed with Lifebuoy soap, Megan's blonde curls were cut off. "Now we can see your lovely skin and the real colour of your hair," the girl said as she took Megan to where Peter and James were waiting, dressed by now.

Poor Peter hadn't had a drink for god knows how long, because he didn't like cocoa, but one of the girls gave him a large enamel mug full of tea which he drank straight down. Normally James would eat and drink anything, but he didn't seem to want much and was very quiet. When the girls asked what was wrong, and why he wasn't eating, Peter told them that during the night he and James were petrified of the old men in the room, especially when one would come to talk, and sit beside James's bed.

James was never the same after that first night in the workhouse. In fact he didn't talk at all for some time after that, and even when speech returned, it returned with a stammer. He also took to pulling his hair out by the handful. Previously, James was always pulling other people's hair out; now it was his turn.

Peter continued to deteriorate, and Reverend Mother had him removed to the hospital wing, to find out what was wrong.

The unmarried mothers were concerned for the children, telling them that it wouldn't be long before they were 'farmed out,' and that it wasn't a proper children's home. Megan got to like the girls, and when they were working in the laundry, Megan would stand on the iron bars of the cots to stroke the babies. "There, there now," she would say, "sister will soon ring the bell, and your mummy will be back."

One day, while the children were in the nursery, Reverend Mother came in and said, "Come along now, I'm going to take you to see Peter, who's sick."

With her lip quivering, Megan said "Can we see Helen? She's sick too."

"Not this time, but you will see her, she's coming on fine, just fine." Reverend Mother took them both by the hand, and out across a great yard, enclosed by a high wall like the exercise yard in a prison. Funny-looking people were walking round it, their heads down, except for one woman, who had big boots on her, and a great long skirt. She was at the pump, pumping the water, even though the bucket she was supposed to be filling was already overflowing. When Reverend Mother and the children got near to her she lifted the bucket of water and threw it all over them. As she stood there laughing, she tried to fill the bucket up again. Then a stout woman in a grey uniform ran over to get her inside.

Reverend Mother brought the children back indoors and handed them over to another nun, saying, "Sarah has thrown water over us."

So Peter's visit was cancelled for another week.

CHAPTER TWO

One week later Reverend Mother came again. "I have a nice surprise for you today," she announced.

"Are we going to see Helen?" Megan asked.

"No, but you will soon – not just yet – soon, yes soon."

When they reached the place where Peter was, not only was he in a room all to himself, but Leonard was there sitting on a chair beside the bed. There was also a little man, sitting with his hat on his knees, and his stick on the back of his chair. "Now then," Reverend Mother said, "I will leave you for a while together."

The little man stood up, and reaching out his arms cried, "You don't know me, do you? Of course you don't, you're too young to remember me," he said as he lifted Megan up.

James tried to say something, but though he opened his mouth, nothing came out. James knew it was Granddad, but Megan couldn't remember much about him.

"What's wrong with you, son?" Granddad asked James.

"He cannot talk any more," Megan shouted, "he got a fright didn't he Peter?"

"What? What fright has he had?" Granddad asked, putting Megan down and picking James up. "Now tell Granddad all about it." But of course, James couldn't.

Though Leonard and Granddad were shocked at what they were seeing, they tried to be cheerful.

"Look," said Granddad, "look what I've brought you." Opening his home-made canvas bag, he brought out sweets and biscuits.

"And what's that in there?" asked Megan, pointing at the honey.

"Oh, that's honey, yes, honey from my own bees."

"Can we have some now?" she pleaded, rummaging through the bag, to see what else he had.

"No," Leonard said, "you have to have honey on bread, you will have it later."

Reverend Mother returned. "Look," Megan said, "we've got honey, Granddad's bees made it. Can we have some now?"

"No," Reverend Mother replied, "later Megan, later. I need to speak to Mr Fay – I mean your grandfather – first." Showing him a letter, she went on to explain, "There's a board meeting in three weeks' time, to decide what is going to happen to the children."

"What's going to happen to them be dammed!" he shouted back, reaching behind for his stick, so as to stand up. "Sure that is why I'm here, I've come to take them out of here, God blast you woman!"

"But Mr Fay, look at you, you are not well yourself, you are a widower, you can hardly look after yourself!"

"There is nothing wrong with me, apart from my old arthritis. Sure I've got enough on my smallholding to feed them, we will manage, won't we, Len?" he added, looking at Leonard.

"Three weeks' time, Mr Fay, you can come to the meeting, and we will see then," she said as she closed the door behind her.

Peter wasn't well enough to talk much, James couldn't talk at all, and only Leonard knew why Granddad was there. When the children were taken away, Leonard had ridden the six miles to Granddad's farm to tell him.

Megan was doing all the talking and listening. "Tell me, Megs," he went on to say, "What did happen to James? Why is he like this?"

"He got a fright," she told him. "He wets himself all the time, he gets told off, he used to speak, now he doesn't. But when he did talk, he used to pull my hair; now he pulls his own hair, and sometimes he puts it in his mouth."

Granddad, by now very disturbed, was finding it very hard not to cry in front of them. Looking over at Leonard, he went on to say, "God Bless us, how much more can I take? First your grandmother, then your mother, my daughter, and your poor father, sure God help him, he couldn't cope without her. Then Helen, but she's coming on grand." Then, looking at Peter, and taking in his thinness, he added, stroking his cheek, "Well, son, we'll fatten you up won't we? We'll get some goats milk down you, and plenty of rabbit stew, and fresh eggs, we'll soon be having you as right as rain."

Leonard wasn't so sure, for he knew Peter had been sick a long time. Even so, he nodded in agreement.

Megan wanted to know more about the bees and the rabbits, and when she could see them.

"I'll tell you what," the old man promised, "Next Sunday I'll come and take you all home to my place for the day. Yes, that's what I'll do, it's only about seven miles from here, I'm sure I'll get you all in the trap."

Reverend Mother came back at this point, to tell them that Peter had had enough for one day.

"I've just told them I'll be coming next Sunday to take them out for the day," Granddad informed her.

Reverend Mother looked surprised and objected that Peter wouldn't be able. Nor was she sure about James: "It may unsettle him," she said. But Megan yes.

"Unsettle him?" the old man shouted back, "Sure look at him, look what this place has done to him!"

Reverend Mother could see the old man was upset and said, "I'm aware of all this Mr Fay, but you must remember, this is a workhouse, not a children's home, we are doing our best."

"Yes," he replied, "I'm sorry, I'm sorry, but try to understand how I am feeling, seeing my daughter's children in here."

"Yes, indeed I do," she tried to reassure him, adding that she hoped the children would see him again soon.

Leonard went back to Granddad's place. On the way back, the old man was very sad and subdued. The silence was broken only when he said, "You'll help me Leonard, won't you, son – I mean to look after them for a while?"

Leonard didn't answer for a while, then said, "What about me farm job? And what about the house? I mean, when Helen is better, she'll want to come home, she'll be fourteen in a few months' time."

The old man reminded Leonard that he had to save the children from being 'farmed out'.

"But Peter's not well, and now look at James," Leonard objected, "James has always been a handful, and now he's worse."

"But Leonard, I must try, your mother and father couldn't rest if I didn't try to help."

"We'll leave it for now," Leonard said, "See how Helen is first. She's a lot better today than she was last week, she's asking to see Megan now, but they won't let her see her yet, in case Megan kicks up when she has to leave."

As Leonard and Granddad arrived back at the old man's cottage, Rover the dog came to meet them, wagging his tail. "Take the shafts off the pony," Granddad told Leonard, "while I go and see how the fire is." On his way in he picked up a few logs, and in no time Leonard could see smoke rising thick from the chimney. "Right lad," the old man said, as he stood at the door. "Open the gate to let the pony into the field, and lay the trap shafts down on them old sacks, you see there. We'll sort all that out later on. Now come and have something to eat and drink, lad, you must be hungry."

But Leonard wasn't hungry; he was worried about Granddad having the children, especially James. Although now James wasn't talking very well, he was pulling his hair out, and Granddad had never seen James in a temper. Leonard knew that even he couldn't control James at times, let alone this little old man.

"We'll manage, won't we Len! Sure you can see I've got enough here, well almost enough with the aul chickens. Plenty of praties and vegetables, and sure look at the aul fruit trees and the bees, sure we will manage – won't we, lad?"

Leonard had been thinking all the time while the old man was on about managing. "Look, Granddad, it's not just the food, it's ... it's, well -"

Before he could finish the old man butted in with, "Sure, that's what it's all about. Food. If ye had enough to eat, sure Helen and Peter wouldn't be sick, and they wouldn't have to be taken away."

"Yes, I know that," Leonard said, "but this place of yours is so small, there isn't enough room for all of us."

"For God's sake lad! Sure your mother was born here, as well as your four aunts, and one uncle. Yes, five of them altogether."

"Well maybe so, Granddad, but Grandma was alive then, and ladies manage better than men, Helen always says. If our mother had lived after our father had died things would be different."

"I know, I know all that, sure your mother had been keeping your family together for years, sure she could put her hands to anything, anything. Like her mother before her, indeed! Like her mother before her ... Minds sharp as a needle they had, as sharp as a needle. Your Grandmother Margaret, could make a meal out of anything. And give her a bale of hay, a ball of string, a pack of needles, a few big sacks, sure she'd make a mattress in no time, sure there was nothing your Grandmother couldn't do."

"That's what I mean," Leonard said, "our mother was the same."

"You don't have to tell me, lad, what your mother could do. Sure your father was a nice easy-going fellow, a good enough chap, but no get-up-and-go. Your mother, my Margaret, could knock him into a hatbox and straight out the other side before he knew he'd been in it. Your father, Lord rest him, would say, 'We will cross that bridge when we come to it,' and when they got to the bridge, your mother not only had to cross the bridge, but also had to pull your father over as well. Your mother was brought up to plan for whatever. You know, lad, what they say, and my God it's true, 'if you fail to plan, you plan to fail.' How true that is, yes indeed! When the good Lord took your mother, He took the heart out of the family, like He does when He takes any good mother. But there now, maybe He thought she'd had enough."

"Granddad, I think you should sit down and think about all this, sit and plan, like you just said."

"But sure, lad, if I had the time I would, they've only given us three weeks, you can see it in that letter, three weeks and then 'farmed out.' Out to where, for God's sake! Yes, where? Might never see them again!"

"Look," Leonard expostulated, "Why don't you have Megan and James here while Peter is sick, and see how you get on with them? I know Megan will be alright, she'll love it here, with Rover and all that, she's no trouble, she's as bright as a button. But on the other hand, she needs another girl, and Helen isn't better yet."

"Go on with you lad, sure I had to manage when your Grandmother died, four girls, yes four of them!"

"Yes, but at least they had each other, and who's going to wash Megan and do her hair? Not that she's got much, now that they've cut her lovely curls off. Helen will go mad when she sees it."

"I think you're right lad, I'll have to give it more thought, I wasn't thinking of anything like that, all I was thinking about was getting them out of there. I'll sleep on it – or will I sleep? I'll ask God to help me sort it out, yes I'll ask God to guide me, to do the right thing, that is, what's best for all of us. Now come with me, lad, while I go and lock the chickens up for the night, and help put the pony away in his shed. Yes, let's lock up for the night, we've had enough, lad, it's been a long day, yes a long day."

"Why are you locking up, grandfather? Sure nobody ever comes around here, the nearest house is about a mile away."

"Well, when I say lock up, you know what I mean, secure the aul henhouse to keep the foxes out. You know lad, them aul foxes can get in anywhere, and they don't just kill one and run, they kill half a dozen or more before they take off with one. Sure I never have a need to buy meat, with that and a rabbit now and again, and not forgetting a few eels. Yes, eels, you can come with me tomorrow, down below in the lane."

"Do you fry them?"

"No, lad, I boil them in salt water, good for ya they are."

"Oh, I don't think I'd like them, I don't even like the look of them!"

"And where would you have seen any eels, lad?" the old man asked.

"Oh, I've seen them outside Mr Burns's shop, along with the

herrings he sells. He keeps eels in a barrel of water, but I've never ate one, don't like the look of them."

"Well, you'll see tomorrow lad, you'll like them when I'm finished with them, a nice bit of butter and a few new praties, washed down with a good mug of buttermilk from Mrs Carter's down the road. You won't have any spots or sores eating my sort of food lad, good aul plain fare, nothing fancy."

As Leonard listened to all this, he was thinking what lovely skin his mother had had, indeed, and how pretty she was. He remembered her being laid out at the wake in her own bedroom, how people were saying then how lovely she looked, how even at forty-two her skin always looked liked peaches and cream. His father would say, "sure mother is a natural beauty, with her natural curly hair, and teeth like pearls." Leonard never saw toothpaste in his house, always a jar of bicarbonate of soda, which was not only used for baking soda bread, but also for cleaning teeth.

That night Leonard heard the screeching of hens being attacked by the fox. He jumped out of bed to get Granddad, but Granddad was already taking his gun down from behind the door. Poor man! Leonard thought as he saw Granddad limping with the gun in one hand and the stick in the other, but by the time they had got to the henhouse, they could see the fox running off with a big white chicken in its mouth.

"There he goes again, run back, lad, and get me the lamp off the trap, we'll see what other damage he's left behind."

When Leonard returned, he could see feathers were still flying everywhere, plus three dead chickens. "But I thought you locked them up safe!"

"I did lad, I did – look!" he replied, pointing to a gap under the wire mesh where the fox had scratched a hole in the soil. "It doesn't matter how hard I try or what I do, that fox gets in. Now you know what they mean when they say 'cunning as a fox.' So now, lad, I'm afraid we'll be having chicken soup tomorrow, instead of eels." Picking up the dead chickens and handing the still warm corpses to Leonard, he continued, "I'll take some down to Carters tomorrow, they'll sell them for me, or they'll give me some tea and sugar, yes a few groceries. Sure, God's good," he muttered once more for the umpteenth time, "Sure God knows what He's doing, it's all sent to try us."

Leonard had never felt so sorry for anyone as he did at that moment, for his old Granddad. Taking the old man's stick, he said, "Come on, Granddad, lean on me, don't worry about that old fox, get yerself in, out of this cold, and I'll help you sort it out tomorrow."

Inside Leonard raked the fire and put a few dry turfs on, that had been laid ready for the morning. Soon the kettle was whistling. "Here," Leonard said, handing the old man a big mug of hot tea, "drink this before you go back to bed, I'll get some more turf in for the morning." As Leonard laid the basket of turf by the side of the fire he watched the old man looking into the flames. "What are you thinking about, Granddad?" he asked.

"Oh well, sure I'm always thinking lad, watching the flames, I'm wondering if they are trying to tell us something, I'm sure they are, if only we could read them, yes indeed they are."

"Well now, Granddad, I'm telling you something. Come on!" Leonard said, taking the old man by the arm, and pulling him from the armchair. "Now back to bed you go, 'cos I'm going to bank this fire up for the night."

"Sure, it's great to have a bit of company," the old man said as he reached for his stick from the back of the chair.

Leonard didn't sleep himself much that night, wondering how he was going to convince the old man that it wouldn't be a good idea for him to take on the children. Sure, he could hardly look after himself.

Next morning as they had breakfast together Leonard said, "Listen Granddad, I still think you should think very carefully about having us all here with you. I can see how hard it is for you to manage on your own."

"Ah, sure it's no trouble, haven't I had to do it before?"

"Well yes, but you were younger then, and you didn't have bad legs and all that."

"I know, I know," the old man replied, "but I'll be alright, you'll see. Don't worry about me. No, lad, don't ever worry about me!"

But Leonard wasn't only worried about him, he was worried about Peter always being sickly. Now Helen had been left with a bad heart, the effect of the rheumatic fever. Now James's nerves were worse than ever, and little Megan, bright as a button, who tried to take care of everyone and everything ... What life would they have here? he asked himself once more, as he looked around the whitewashed, stone-walled cottage. And with no neighbours in sight of a mile.

For a few days Leonard stayed and helped his Granddad, taking in the life of the place. He watched as the old man struggled to get water from the well, boil up potatoes and meal for the chickens, milk the two goats, and tend the bit of vegetable garden – and of course the bees. Yes, the bees. Leonard laughed when he saw what the old man did when he had to get the honey out. Granddad had an old galvanised bucket with holes in it, that he would put on his head, and on top of that he put an old net curtain. This, he said, stopped the bees from getting at him, and indeed it worked.

The day before Leonard was due to go home the old man said, "Them old boots of yours need repairing, give them here lad. I noticed the soles are not too good when you bent down at the well. Is that the only boots ya have?"

"Well, yes," Leonard replied.

"Right, lad, see that last over there behind the door and the old tin box beside it? Bring them over here, then go down to the shed. You'll see some old bicycle tyres hung up, bring me one."

The old man cut a piece off the tyre and laid it on the floor. Then he laid the boot on top, so as to measure it. Next he took a knife from his tin box, sharpened it on the stone doorstep, and cut out the shape of the boots. He set the boots on the last, then hammered on the new soles, rubber side out, with tacks which he held in his mouth.

"Job complete," he told Leonard. "Now you will never have

wet feet again, and them soles won't ever wear out, the uppers will go first."

And he was proved right, and that was the first time Leonard found out that his Grandfather was indeed a cobbler by trade. Leonard learned many things from the old man during his few days there, but could never see himself living like this or indeed trying to – it was too much like hard work, as he told Helen when he went to see her and to tell her that she would be coming back to live with him, and that James would be going to Artane. Peter still wasn't well enough to go anywhere, and little Megan would be going to New Town Forbe to be looked after by nuns.

"Does Grandfather know all this?" asked Helen, "He won't like it that James is going to Artane. Those Christian Brothers in Artane will kill him because of his temper."

"I know that," Leonard replied, "but apparently, the home had a meeting. Grandfather went, and I suppose they could see how he could hardly manage himself, also they sent someone out to look at the place."

"Poor Grandfather!" Helen said as she wiped her tears, "God help him, he did try. Have you seen him since?"

"Yes I have, and he said that he's not giving up, especially on James. In no way, he told them was James going to Artane. But he wasn't as polite as that."

"Poor Grandfather!" Helen repeated. She always called him 'Grandfather,' as she felt she was too old to say Granddad.

In those days no one knew how serious rheumatic fever could be, or indeed that it left scars, so Helen left Hospital and returned home to live with Leonard, trying to manage on Leonard's 10s per week, plus 2/6 she earned doing a bit of domestic work, which she should not have been doing in her state.

Granddad won his case and got James, and later Peter. Megan went to the nuns, but would be allowed home to Granddad's farm for weekends, and sometimes longer. The boys' spell of living with Granddad was brief, and it was on one of Leonard's visits there that Granddad talked for the first time about his only son. Ben had never really been mentioned before, except to say that he was married and had four brats of children who wrecked the place when they visited. That had included pulling the unripened apples and pears from the trees and throwing them at each other. As Granddad told Leonard, it wasn't easy to bring children up properly. "Yes indeed, anyone can drag children up, but bringing them up right and proper is jolly hard work." However, he went on to tell Leonard what he had in mind, knowing it would be no use asking Leonard to come and live here, as the authorities wouldn't allow it. Now he told Leonard that his son was living a few miles away, and that his son's place was even smaller than his own.

"God!" Leonard exclaimed, "And they've got four children, how and where do they all sleep?"

"Well," the old man replied, "As long as they are man and wife, the authorities don't ask where all the children sleep."

"What about all the families with ten, twelve, sometimes more? Most people only have two bedrooms, look at your own mother and father with eight of you altogether."

" I never knew we had more."

"Oh yes indeed, there was another James who died at birth, and of course Peter, who also died at birth."

Leonard said, "I did use to hear Brigit -"

Before he could finish this sentence Granddad interrupted him, saying, "That older sister of yours has a lot to answer for. Your poor mother wasn't cold in her grave, when she took herself off to Belfast, leaving your poor father to care for Megan, only a baby. And of course the rest of you. And I don't suppose you ever hear from her, either."

"No, but I think Helen knows where she is in Belfast."

"You know," Granddad went on, "that girl never came up for her own father's funeral."

"I know," Leonard said, "but maybe she didn't know he had died, and we didn't know where she was."

"Oh, don't make excuses for her, lad, she was eighteen years old, she should have known better, but never mind that. This is what I've got to tell you. You see, lad, I'm not very well, and I'm finding it very hard to get about, and I'm worried about the boys. So, I've had talks with Ben, and this is what we've come up with. I'm going to live in Ben's little place and he's going to move in here. I've told him that in return for looking after the boys, I'll sign the lot over to him. It's all my own, lock, stock and barrel. I was going to leave it to you when I die. I don't think you would want to live here, but you could have sold it. It's not worth a great deal, but there's the bit of land around it."

"What about James and Peter? You know what a handful James is, does Ben's wife know that?"

"Well, what else can I do, lad? I know what James is like, now. Sure he's always battering poor Peter, and he hates the village school down below. That boy needs help of some sort, but sure I'm not able any more. No, I'm not able any more, but at least I did stop James going to Artane."

Now Granddad was living alone again, coming now and again to see the boys. Ben was beating hell out of James, and James was beating hell out of the rest of the children, and refusing to go to school. Leonard was sent for, and told to take James home with him, or James would be put away. By now Granddad was too ill to interfere, and was no longer able to visit, but Leonard noticed that his orchard, of which he had been so proud and where he had kept his bees, had been wrecked. The hives were no longer there.

Peter was once again very pale. He knew why Leonard had been sent for, and asked to be taken home with him as well, as Ben's children kept pinching him, and mocking James's stammer. Ben and his shrewish wife Lana seemed pleased when Leonard said that he was taking Peter home as well, and Lana lost no time flinging their few belongings into a bag, saying, "Mr Dunn's bus will be along in ten minutes. If you hurry, you'll catch it."

They did catch the bus.

For a while Leonard thought that coming home was changing James for the better, but not for long. Leonard was now getting only 5 shillings Orphans Pension for the boys, 2/6 each. No one came to find out why they had moved, and Leonard didn't volunteer anything to anyone. The boys' school was right opposite their house so that wasn't a problem, but food and clothes were, especially when Helen told Leonard that she too was going to Belfast as soon as she could get the fare.

Before Helen took off for Belfast, Leonard decided to visit Granddad. He cycled the eight miles only to find the place empty. Perhaps he'd gone to live with Uncle Ben, he thought, but as he cycled the further four miles he began to doubt it. For a start Grandad couldn't stand Lana, – or those 'brats,' as he used to call them. Moreover, it would break his heart to see the mess they had made of his place. Then Leonard reflected that maybe Granddad was so ill that he no longer cared. Whatever, he had to find out.

As he opened the gate into the drive one of Ben's daughters came running up to him, saying, "We're moving to Monaghan!"

Ignoring this news, Leonard asked, "Where's Granddad, where's Granddad?"

"He's sick," she replied, "he's in the County Home." For a moment Leonard thought he was hearing things. "He's sick," she repeated, "he's in the County Home."

When Leonard got inside the house, he could see why Granddad didn't like 'that Lana', as he called her. He had never taken much notice of her the few times he had seen her before, but as he looked at her now, he knew what Granddad meant when he said she was coarse, uncouth and ill-mannered to put it mildly.

"If you're looking for your Granddad, he's in the County Home," she greeted him.

Leonard felt like saying, 'Isn't he your children's grandfather also?' but he thought better of it, and as she hadn't noticed how wet he was or indeed offered him so much as a cup of tea, let alone enquired after himself or the children, he decided to return home.

But before he left, he said, "Mary says you're moving to Monaghan."

"Yes, that's right," she confirmed without looking up from what she was doing. "Yes, as soon as we sell this place, we're off, and that'll be soon we hope. Yes, very soon."

As Leonard cycled home, he couldn't stop thinking what a strange turning this life had taken. Now poor Granddad had become one of those fearsome and pathetic creatures that had frightened the life out of Megan and James, leaving James a nervous wreck. Leonard could no longer hold back his tears, and cycled home openly crying in his helplessness.

"Guess what, Helen, guess where they have put Granddad! His only son, Ben, and that awful wife, no wonder Granddad couldn't ever take to her!"

"Calm down, Leonard, it cannot be that bad."

"It is," he said, "he's in the workhouse, or the County Home, whatever you like to call it."

"My God!" Helen exclaimed, "just where we've been, why is he there?"

"He's sick, that woman said."

Helen realised what that meant. "That means he won't come out until ... " At that Leonard broke down again. "Here, drink this," Helen said, handing him a mug of tea, "and get that wet coat off you, or you will be -" She stopped herself.

"I don't care if I do die," Leonard said. "Granddad doesn't deserve what they've done to him."

By now they were all crying, and James shouted, "I'll go and kill them!"

A little later James enquired, "Will Granddad have all his hair cut off? And will he be wearing one of those striped shirts?"

Leonard confirmed that that was what they did in there, and the thought of it made James repeat his vow to going over to kill "Granddad's son, and that aul bitch Lana." No one calls Ben uncle.

"Be quiet James," Helen said, "Granddad wouldn't want you to talk like that."

Leonard was Granddad's only visitor at the workhouse, for although all the children wanted to see him, there was no money for bus fares. He cycled the eight miles there and back every Sunday to see him, but towards the end of his life Granddad no longer recognised him, which was very upsetting. Shortly after that he died, and although Granddad had daughters scattered around Northern Ireland as well as his son Ben, Leonard didn't know where any of them were. Thus he was the only member of his family to attend the funeral, which had to be paid for by the Society of St Vincent De Paul, as the family had no money.

Leonard did go back to Granddad's old house to see if he could find where Ben had moved to. The new people there said all that they knew was that Ben had moved to Monaghan and left no forwarding address.

CHAPTER THREE

Before Helen left for Belfast, she and Leonard decided to have another try at getting Megan out of the convent. Poor Megan hated life there, and every letter she wrote contained the plea, 'When are you coming for me, Helen?' Helen realised that whatever slim chance she might have of getting Megan home whilst she was there, Leonard would have no chance at all of getting her out once she'd left for Belfast.

In the small town where they lived – indeed, in the same street – the children had quite a few relatives, but all were like themselves; poor, with large families. None of them could help, as they had nothing to spare from their own continuous fight for survival. But Mary Murray, whose family was related to them on their father's side, told Helen that if it would help she would say that she was prepared to keep an eye on Megan. "I'll say anything as long as it helps to get Megan out," she promised.

"That would be great, Mary," Helen said gratefully. "I know you're struggling yourself, and I know you can't afford to feed another mouth, so we won't be bothering you in that way – but if I go to Belfast leaving her in the home, she'll be there for years."

Thus, after much toing and froing, Megan was allowed to return home.

Helen gave Len two shillings for Megan's bus fare. He himself cycled the eight miles to the home to collect Megan, whom he found waiting on the steps of the convent with a nun. When she saw Len she was so eager to leave, she couldn't even wait to say goodbye to the nun, and Len had to make her go back to say thank you. In his mind Len was thinking that maybe one day, Megan might have to return. God forbid, but one never knows, he said to himself.

She and Len waited for Donnelly's bus, that passed the convent every day at 3.30pm. Once he had seen her onto the bus, he told Mr Donelly to drop her off outside the house. "You know where we live Mr Donelly, don't you?"

"Sure, everyone knows you! Sure I knew your poor father well, Lord rest him."

Megan sat on the seat right behind Mr Donnelly and never stopped talking throughout the journey.

Once she got to house she expected to see Helen, but Helen was still in work in Reilly's, and had no control over her hours; she finished at whatever time they chose to let her go. It made no difference how many hours she worked, it was still only 2/6 per week plus her food, and sometimes she'd be given a bit of left-over food for James and Peter.

The house was cold and damp, with a paraffin lamp or candles for light, but Megan didn't care because at last she was home again with Helen. Poor Helen should not have been doing such heavy domestic work, which included carrying buckets of water from a pump about a quarter of a mile away. She was also sometimes expected to take the Reilly children into the fields for picnics, and when this happened she would include Megan as an unofficial guest, and feed her until she couldn't eat any more. Helen had no qualms about this; knew the Reilly children wouldn't go hungry as their family owned a shop that sold everything from paraffin to perfume, including their own fresh milk and butter.

After Megan had been home a few months Helen left for Belfast, to better herself as she hoped. She knew Megan would be upset, but felt she had to make the break, as she could see no future living where she was. Before she left she warned James not to beat Megan, nor indeed Peter who was getting thinner and thinner. Meanwhile, Megan went to the local convent school, which was run by the Sisters of Mercy, but the only sign of mercy in the regime lay in the name, which was also taken by several of the nuns as their vocational name.

Megan was a chatty little soul, and would talk to anybody, including cats and dogs – and indeed there were plenty of both running around, just as hungry as herself. She had become quite streetwise, and all the shopkeepers knew her and liked her, for however cold and hungry she was she never stopped smiling and was always willing to run errands, or 'messages', as they were called in those days, in return for pennies or cuts of bread. Often people would give her a choice, but after a short while at school with the Sisters of Mercy she could no longer accept the bread; she needed the pennies to buy her schoolbooks, for in those days books weren't free, but must be bought with what she could earn by running messages and carrying buckets of water from the well, as there was no mains supply to the village.

As well as having to buy her books she, like ever other child, had to contribute five shillings per year towards the heating of the school. So, because she had no chance of finding all that money all at once, as well as running messages to buy her books she now had to stay in after school to sweep the classrooms: the cash being unavailable, the nuns regarded such child-labour as acceptable payment in kind. It was quite a formal instalment plan, and all the other children knew why Megan was sweeping the classrooms; Sister Conception, the nun in charge, kept accounts, and would record on the blackboard for the benefit of whoever might be interested Megan's progress towards her target of five shillings. By way of additional incentive, she could expect to have her ears boxed should she fall behind.

On one occasion Duffy's circus came to town, and Megan paid sixpence to go. The next day she was so excited at having seen the clowns and the performing animals that she told Sister Eucaria, a nun from Bundorran who taught Irish, all about her experience. For this the nun battered Megan about the ears – "How dare you go to the Circus, when you don't even have an Irish textbook?" She battered Megan some more when Megan responded that learning Irish was no good, "because everybody is going to England anyway."

It was Sister Eucaria's pleasure to pick on a poor, vulnerable child every day. She enjoyed pulling their ears and otherwise humiliating them in front of the class. Those poor children who went barefoot would be sent out to wash their feet, which in winter meant having to break the ice first. Most of the poor children, especially those who had mothers, would be kept at home when the weather was that bad, but Megan had no choice, whatever the weather, because Helen had told her she must never miss school; otherwise she would be sent back to the orphanage.

Nor did Sister Eucaria ever let Megan forget who she was. She approached her, as she approached all poor children, with a grimace, as if a bad smell had suddenly wafted under her nose. Whatever Megan's behaviour, she never failed to tell her that her mother was looking down on her, and grieving at her naughtiness. But not all the nuns were like her, and Megan did enjoy mathematics and cookery, probably because the two nuns who taught her for those subjects were kind.

She had the Reverend Mother herself for maths, and maybe the nun realised that Megan had a quick mind. But for whatever reason Megan did very well at maths.

Sister Theresa was a tall, elegant, kind-faced nun in her twenties, who taught other subjects besides cookery. She took an interest in Megan, and in return Megan showed a great liking for cookery. In class she would ask every time if she could cook, and Sister Theresa would say, "But you cooked last time Megan. Besides, will you be able to get the ingredients?"

"Of course I will," she would reply, "and if I can't get them, I'll ask one of the shopkeepers if they want me to cook for them."

This she did many times, and some of the shopkeepers would say when she returned with whatever she had made, "Now, Megan, do you want paying for this or would you like to keep it for yourself?"

Of course, they knew very well that she would share it with Peter and James. Sometimes it was hard to know what she should do for the best, whether to take the money or the food. It depended on what was in the house. If she had no light to do her homework, she would have the money for candles, and if she had neither food nor candles, she would do her homework under the street light outside her house. Either way, she must do it, or face a battering next day. Homework was hardest in the winter, because by the time she got home from school after sweeping the classrooms it would be almost dark.

It was on a day when she was getting a battering from 'Chew Bees Face' as Sister Eucaria was called, that Sister Theresa called Megan over after class and said, "Now, Megan don't cry." She went on to tell her that the Sister wasn't well and that Megan must pray for her. She herself would pray with her.

As they were praying under the statue of the Blessed Virgin, Megan glanced up at Sister Theresa and saw silent tears rolling down her face.

Another shopkeeper who was kind to her was Mrs Dogherty, who had the bakery. Her cake-making days were every Tuesday and Friday, and Megan would stand outside looking into the window until Mrs Dogherty noticed her, and beckoned her inside. She would invite her to choose six cakes, which she would put in a paper bag and say, "Now run and share them with James and Peter." Mrs Dogherty would also tell Megan to bring the milk can down so that she could fill it with fresh milk.

Other shopkeepers would give her old clothes, which she would shorten by cutting down the hems and sleeves. Usually she left them ragged, but sometimes, when she could afford the sewing cotton (or 'thread' as it was called in those days) she would sew them with a proper hem. But as she lacked the skill to take them in properly, the effect was always very baggy. Everyone knew she had been given the clothes, but she didn't mind – even if she was given a hat she would wear it – and as she was always talking to the shopkeepers, they called her 'the little street urchin'. But for Megan's exertions, Peter would not have lived as long as he did.

Megan collected the Orphans' pension on Fridays before going to school. To be sure of not being late, she would wait for Mrs Dunn to open the post office. Then she would go next door to Donaghoes' with her seven and sixpence to buy bread and milk, so that she and the boys could have something to eat before school. She would ask Mrs Donaghoe to hold the rest of the money until she came from school when she would spend it. As they generally had no fire the food always had to be things that didn't need cooking, so it ran largely to bread, milk, tea and sugar, as any of the neighbours in the street would boil a kettle for them. It was only on Saturday and Sunday nights that the fire was lit, because Len got paid each Saturday evening.

He would have cycled the six miles home with a sack of turf (given to him by the farmer) tied to his old bike. Megan would be waiting for him at the bottom of the hill, and he would always give her the ten shilling note, saying, "Get what you can with it, Megan."

By that time the shops were always closed, but Megan would go to the shopkeepers' back doors saying, "I'm sorry I'm late, but Len has just got home." After the first few times she didn't have to say it any more, the shopkeepers just accepted it. Her first call was on Mr Mackin the butcher. Mr Mackin wouldn't bother to weigh the two shillings' worth of sausages she'd ask for. He would cut a big chain from the sausages that hung from the ceiling, and as he bagged them up he would say, "I suppose you want some suet to fry them in?"

"Yes please," she would reply. From the butcher, she would go to Donaghoe's, where she'd buy sugar, tea, two loaves, milk and candles. There was never any jam, cakes or biscuits, though Mrs. Donaghoe would sometimes put butter in the bag. By the time Megan got back home, Leonard would have the kettle boiling on a turf fire he had lit.

Their only food for the weekend was this big pan of sausages on Saturday night and the rest on the Sunday. Sausages and more sausages.

Although James was a bully he was also a coward. Consequently, when the dentists made their rounds of the schools James refused treatment and didn't turn up, leaving poor Megan to stand alone in the queue. Other children had their mothers to support them, but she had no one, even though she had a couple of back teeth removed.

Because she and James often suffered from sore throats, the school doctor decided that their tonsils must come out, so one Sunday a van turned up out of the blue and whipped Megan off the street. James ran off once again. A few days later Megan was dumped back in the same spot where she had been picked up.

Her throat felt terrible, and there was no one to comfort her with warm drinks, let alone ice cream. NOTHING.

Megan was still so deathly afraid of the Orphanage that she agreed to everything which was demanded of her, including going back to school the very day after being dumped on the street, but she felt so sick there that she laid her head down on the desk. It got her no sympathy, only a prod in the back with the pointer from Chew Bees Face – "Wake up, you lazy child!"

But despite all this Megan never felt sorry for herself. She had one close friend in little Jayne Carters, who was just two days younger, and lived a few doors away from her, and whose father was Megan's godfather. But poor John Carters couldn't help Megan because of his own big family, and in fact himself died very young, leaving three children still at school, including Jayne. Jayne's mother was a hard-working woman – she had to be to keep food on the table, for if she wasn't out in the back yard scrubbing clothes on the washboard, she would be baking cheap, nourishing food, such as soda bread or potato bread.

Megan envied Jayne, for even though they were also poor, Jayne had a mother, and there was always smoke coming out of the chimney, and paraffin to keep the lamps burning. As she told Jayne, these three things were very important to Megan. Megan also envied Jayne because when it was very cold Mrs Carters would keep the children away from school, and Megan would see them looking out of the window, as she went by in her bare feet in the snow. Jayne once asked Megan if it was cold walking in your bare feet in the snow; Megan replied, "Only when you stop, but if you keep walking or better still run, you don't feel the cold so much."

Jayne also had grown-up sisters who helped out by doing some domestic work for shopkeepers, but even so, Mrs Carters was a good mother who always managed to keep smoke coming out of the chimney, plus lights in the house.

But hail, rain, blow or snow, Megan had to turn up for school, although sometimes she found it hard going, especially when the cold and hunger had kept her from sleeping the night before. Even then she was likely to get beaten for not having the appropriate books. Consequently, apart from maths she didn't learn much at school, and says now that a child who is cold, hungry and frightened will never be able to take in what is set before her. It was only years later, whilst in service in Belfast with a kind English family, that Megan, with the help of her mistress, taught herself the rudiments of English grammar, spelling, etc.

Christmas was getting near, and Megan and Jayne were looking in the window of Mr Cosgrove's toyshop, when Megan said, "See that doll up there?"

"Yes," said Jayne.

"Well, I'm having that for Christmas."

"Don't be silly," Jayne said, "who have you got to buy you that?"

"I'm buying it myself, just like my shoes, that I'm buying in Tierney's. Come over to Tierney's window, and I'll show you."

They ran over the street to Tierney's, and pointing to a lovely pair of brown shoes, Megan said, "There, that's what I'm buying. Bet?"

"You're not!"

"Bet I am!"

"Bet you're not!"

"You'll see, Jayne."

Every spare penny she earned from running messages and carrying buckets of water from the pump, Megan gave either to Mrs Tierney or to Mr Cosgrove, who would then write it on the lid of the shoe or doll box, until, finally, on the night of Christmas Eve, she had the last necessary pennies. The shops had closed by the time she had carried her last buckets of water. Mr Cosgrove, who wasn't known for his liking of the poor, wouldn't open the back door when Megan called, just shouted, "We're closed!" But then, he came from a priestly family, and he was a great one for visiting the presbytery, to gossip and play tennis.

Earlier the same day, one of those same priests, who likewise wasn't noted for having much time for the poor of the town, had caught James and Peter in the church grounds next door looking for a few sticks to start the turf fire. He not only took the sticks off them, but boxed their ears as well. This particular priest was known to come from a rich family, and was often seen riding to hounds, or playing tennis with the bankers and the Cosgroves. He also directed the choir practice in the church, where James sang. Even though James had a bad stammer when speaking, when he sang there was never a flaw in his voice – indeed, he had a lovely singing voice, as did Helen. Even so James knew there was no point asking if he could join the choir.

That priest would walk past their house every day to say Mass, not knowing who they were, never speaking or even knowing they were orphans, fighting for survival. Priests nowadays are no longer like this, thank God, nor the nuns I believe. The religious life is no longer so much easier and more prosperous than that of ordinary people.

But Mrs Tierney was different, she didn't mind Megan knocking late on Christmas Eve to collect her shoes. "Oh there you are, Megan," she said, "I was worried you would be afraid to come round the back way." Mrs Tierney went upstairs and left Megan sitting in the lovely warm kitchen, which had a splendid great range, with pots boiling on it, and was blazing with electric lights.

When she returned Megan noticed a list of pennies and twopences as long as your arm written all over the lid of the box. "My God, Megan," Mrs Tierney said, "I hope these aren't all buckets of water on this lid!"

"No, Mrs Tierney," she said smiling as usual in her bare feet.

"Now, Megan, have you got any socks or stockings?"

"No, but I'll be alright," said Megan.

"Well, I didn't think you would have any socks or stocking, seeing you in your bare feet, so I've put two pairs of stockings in the box with yer shoes."

"Oh, thank you Mrs Tierney, thanks!" said Megan, but Mrs Tierney noticed the hesitancy in her voice.

"So, Megan, what are you trying to tell me? That you can't pay me for the stockings, perhaps?"

"Well, yes – but I will pay you after Christmas."

"Oh I don't want paying for them stockings, you have them on me for Christmas, just give me the ninepence you owe me on your shoes."

"What I was trying to tell you, Mrs Tierney, is that I will need elastic to keep my stockings up."

"Of course you will," she said, and immediately shouted up to her husband to bring down a card of elastic. "There you are Megan, I'll cut it for you, and you can tie it yourself. By the way, did you get that doll you were telling me about across at Cosgroves?"

"No, I didn't – I was late, he doesn't stay open late, like the other shops that sell food. I did go to his back door, he was in but wouldn't open the door."

"Oh never mind, maybe it's because he hasn't got children of his own, or he'd forgot you were coming."

"Oh, I don't mind, Mrs Tierney, I've got my shoes haven't I?"

"Indeed you have, Megan. Goodnight now, and Happy Christmas."

Megan still felt she had won her bet with Jayne, but thought to herself, I bet Jayne isn't having sausages for Christmas dinner. Jayne's mother kept a few hens and grew her own vegetables. Megan used to hear people say that Christmas was a sad time, and that the cold and hunger of January and February would wipe out a lot of people. Indeed, she was beginning to notice a lot of people dying. Among the poor of Ireland in those days, it was the custom when someone died to nail a big, black lace bow to the front door. That meant that there was a wake being held, and anyone could go in to pay last respects to the dead person, who would be laid out in bed in a brown habit. People would go in and say to the bereaved family, "Sorry for your troubles," then kneel by the bed and say a prayer. The grown-ups would take a pinch of snuff, which would be on a table by the side of the bed, and they would also be given a cup of tea.

Megan had no idea why the snuff was always provided, but whenever she saw the black bow on someone's door she went in. Although she often knew the person who had been laid out, she didn't enjoy seeing them dead; all she went in for was the tea and biscuits. She would walk in, say, "Sorry for your troubles," to the bereaved and shake hands with them. Then she would be shown into the room, hoping there would be other people there; if not she would get out quick, after her tea and biscuit.

James would never go in, but would tell Megan, "Did you know So-and-so has died?"

There was plenty of deaths after Christmas that year, and Megan thought Peter was going to be one of them, from consumption, as pulmonary tuberculosis was called in those days. It was also called TB, or Tea and Bread, after the poor diet of the poor people who were its main victims.

That January, while it was still cold and dark, Megan often came home from school after sweeping, clutching a penny candle to do her homework, to find James sitting on the steps. He often sat there, because since his fright in the workhouse he disliked being indoors in the dark. So he sat there, looking at the street lamp for company.

"Where's Peter?" Megan asked.

"He's up in the room. He's sick."

"How long has he been there?"

"Oh, I don't know."

Megan lit the candle and went to see Peter, whom she found lying on the hay mattress that she and Peter had made a few weeks earlier from four flour sacks Leonard had brought home from the farm. Megan's friend Jayne had lent her a big pack-thread needle belonging to her mother, a pair of scissors and a ball of string. She had cut open the four sacks, sewn two together for each side of the mattress, then stuffed it with hay, also provided by Jayne from her mother's shed. They made the mattress for Peter, because James was still wetting the bed.

Megan shouted for James because she thought Peter was dead, "Get some water from the Gallon!"

James came in, whimpering as usual. Although he was a bully, he was no good in a crisis, and he started crying at the sight of Peter's black curls on the pillow.

Helen had always told Megan to pray. "God will hear you," she said. 'Please God help me,' she prayed, while aloud she shouted, "My God, James, Peter is just like Helen was! Get Mrs Smith from next door."

Mrs Smith didn't come, but her grown up son Tom, who at the time was a sanitary inspector, did. "I don't know what's wrong with Peter," he said, "I'll have to get the doctor." Looking around the room and recognising a bowl on the window sill, Tom Smith added, "Has my mother been in here?"

"Yes," James said, "She's been bringing soup to Peter."

Megan knew everyone in the town, and knew that on this particular evening, the Saint Vincent De Paul Society would be holding their annual meeting in the church hall. So she ran around to the church hall and banged on the door, and when they didn't open it at once, she ran home, and tearing a page from her exercise book, she wrote: 'My Brother Peter is dying, I need help. Meg Glyn'.

Then she ran back and pushed it under the church hall door. Once again she ran back home, only to see Peter being loaded into a van similar to the one that had previously been used to take them to the workhouse.

About 9.30 that same night, after the meeting in the church hall was over, one of the members of St Vincent De Paul came and asked about Peter. Megan told him that Peter had been taken away, at which he gave Megan a food voucher for 5 shillings.

Peter was diagnosed with typhoid, but nobody knew for sure how he got it. Was it the conditions he was living in? If so why didn't the others get typhoid also? Peter was asthmatic in any case, he was also very undernourished and always sickly. But Tom Smith knew that his mother was a carrier of typhoid, which was why he asked if she had been there.

The same time that Peter was taken away Mrs Smith went missing also.

When a neighbour told Megan that Mrs Smith was a carrier of typhoid she commented, "That's why we never see Mrs Smith at the shops."

Megan had thought it was because Mrs Smith had her grown-up family living with her and that she didn't need to do her own messages. "Now you've said it she's always walking alone to and from Mass," Megan replied.

No one was allowed to visit Peter for some time, and meanwhile the house was fumigated. But apart from that no one took much notice and certainly didn't stop James and Megan carrying on as normal. That is, apart from James hitting Megan, now that Peter wasn't there to protect her.

Megan decided it was time she visited Peter, so one Saturday morning she got on Donnelly's bus and paid her two shillings, saying to Mr Donnelly, "I'm paying a shilling to go and another to come back, two shillings altogether."

"I suppose you're going to see Peter."

"I am," she said.

"Well keep your florin, Megan, and buy something from me for Peter."

"Oh, I've got him sweets," she said showing him the paper bag in her hand.

"Well keep it – I mean the money."

"Thank you Mr Donnelly, thank you!" Megan passed the rest of the journey sitting behind Mr Donnelly talking non-stop, telling him all about Peter's typhoid, and the house being disinfected, and that Mrs Smith had given Peter typhoid, and how now Mrs Smith was also missing.

"Is that so, and how did she give him typhoid?"

"Oh I don't know, but she could hear him cough in the room above. And she would bring him in soup for his asthma and all that."

"So Mrs Smith is a nice lady then?"

"Oh yes, she's a very nice lady, she used to tell us stories about our mother."

"Did she now?"

"Yes, our mother did sewing for her, and she would give us chickens and eggs."

"Did she now?"

"Yes she did. The Smiths buy and sell chickens, and sometimes we can hear them killing the chickens, especially at Christmas, and kid goats too, we could hear them cry."

"Here we are then, Megan. And, Megan, make sure you're here no later than half past three."

"I will, Mr Donnelly, don't you worry, I will."

Megan often wondered what the nurses thought of the scruffy little girl saying, "I've come to see my brother," for in those days there were no formal visiting hours.

"What's your name?" the nurse asked.

"Meg Glyn," she replied. "My brother is Peter and he has typhoid. Mrs Smith gave it to him and he's also got asthma." The nurse took her by the hand and took her into a room where Peter was propped up among loads of pillows. His poor face was as white as the bed-sheets, and almost all his lovely black curls had now gone. Even so, Megan could tell by the look in his big brown eyes he was pleased to see her.

"Now Peter," the nurse said, "Isn't this grand? Your little sister has come to see you. Well, Megan, would you like to feed Peter while I go and get some milk? And would you like some? Or you can have some rice."

"Yes please, I'll have the rice."

While the nurse had gone Megan tried to spoon the rice into Peter's mouth, but each time Peter would push the spoon away, pointing to Megan's mouth meaning for her to have it, knowing all too well that she might not have had any food that day.

The nurse returned with a big bowl of rice for Megan and tea for Peter. "Your brother loves his tea, doesn't he? Would you like some tea, yourself?"

"No, thank you, I don't like tea on its own, only when I'm eating bread, so I'll just have the milk thank you."

"Well now, sure if you'd like some tea, you can have bread as well."

Peter seemed pleased that Megan was being fed. "Look," the nurse said, "that's the first time I've seen him smile. You've enjoyed that rice, tea and bread?"

"Yes, thank you."

"What have you had to eat today?"

"Sweets," Megan replied, "I got them for Peter when I got our pension from Mrs Dunn's, so I ate some."

"Do you always buy sweets from your pension?"

"Oh no, just today for Peter."

"What time's your bus?"

"Half three."

"You've got a long wait, haven't you?"

"Yes, but I don't mind."

The nurse looked concerned. "I think we'll leave Peter to have a rest now. You come with me. Now then, have you had enough to eat, and do you want to go to the toilet? I mean do you want to do wee wee?"

"No," Megan said.

"But I think you'd better," the nurse said, "because you have a long wait."

Just then Megan saw Mrs Smith go out the door and into the hospital grounds, where she walked around in her black shawl, saying her Rosary. "That's Mrs Smith!" Megan shouted.

Just then Mrs Smith turned round and saw Megan. "How's Peter," she asked, putting her arms around Megan and kissing her on her mouth. Megan spent some time with Mrs Smith, and neither of them mentioned typhoid.

"So you know that lady?" another nurse enquired.

"Yes, she's Mrs Smith and she lives next door to us. She tells us lots of stories about our Mother, and she's a carrier of typhoid."

"Is she now, and how do you know that?"

"Everyone knows that. She gave Peter typhoid."

"How's Peter?" Mr Donnelly asked.

"He's sick."

"Sure, I know he's sick. Is he getting better?"

"I don't know, he is very white and thin, and he didn't eat his rice."

"Ah, sure don't worry yourself, he's in the right place and he'll be coming home in no time, you'll see."

"I miss Peter, Mr Donnelly, he stops James from hitting me."

Sadly, Peter died shortly after that conversation, aged twelve years.

James went on beating Megan, and Leonard was worried, because people were talking. Then one day Leonard came home and thought it strange that Megan wasn't waiting in her usual position at the bottom of the hill to collect his ten shillings and do the weekend messages. James was nowhere to be seen either.

Megan could have been in any of the houses on the hill, for even though the people hadn't a lot themselves, at least she could get warm now and again. There were Tommy and Kathleen Flaherty, whom Megan thought a lot of because Tommy had given her the money for the circus, the Murrays, the Smiths, the Gaffneys and of course Jayne Carters and nice Mrs Martin – they all kept an eye out for Megan.

Leonard went from door to door looking for Megan, and found her at last in Mrs Martin's house, with both eyes closed by bruises. "Jesus Christ," he expostulated, "who's done that to you?"

"Who do you think?" said Mrs Flaherty, who was also present.

"I'll kill him!" Leonard said.

"You kill him, if you can," Kathleen Flaherty said, "But you'll have to catch him before I do, the bully."

Leonard didn't go looking for James as he knew that even though he was a bully, he was also frightened of the unknown and the dark. Sooner or later he would be back, but to teach him a lesson, Leonard bolted the door, knowing he would be frightened outside on his own. When James was finally let in, Leonard belted hell out of him, asking him why he did it. James replied, "She always sings when I sing, she should sing her own songs."

"One of these days you'll kill her," Leonard said. Although he had belted hell out of him, he felt sorry for James, what with his stammering and the conditions they were living in.

CHAPTER FOUR

It was then that Mrs Martin decided to take Megan into her own house. Mrs Martin was well known in the town, and greatly respected for her kindness to the poor. Over the years all sorts of stories went around about Mrs Martin's past, and Megan got to know her better than anyone else. That was how she came to learn the true story from Mrs Martin's own lips.

Mrs Martin's maiden name had been Kane, and her parents had moved from Northern Ireland and bought a business, which had thrived under them. Mary Kane and her brother Charles were sent away to boarding school, and from there Mary was sent to finishing school in France. She still spoke fluent French, and liked to tell Megan stories about her time there. Meanwhile Charles went onto Trinity College, Dublin where he qualified as a doctor. Then, in the same year that he qualified, he died of Brights disease.

Soon after Mary returned from finishing school, she ran off to Scotland with one of her father's workmen, a man called Charlie Martin. The stress of losing first his son and now his daughter was too much for Mr Kane to bear; it caused him to have a stroke from which he never fully recovered.

In those days all medical bills were met privately, if you were lucky enough to be able to meet them at all. A live-in nurse was brought in to look after her father, twenty-four hours a day, but meanwhile the man to whom her father had entrusted his business proved to be far from trustworthy. When this came out Mr Kane had yet another stroke and died. Whilst all this was going on Mary, who had married Charlie Martin in Scotland, was discovering his true character. He had taken to beating her up. Her father had disowned her before he died, and cut her out of his will, so she was left with none of her expected inheritance, much to Charlie Martin's disgust as he liked a drink.

As a result of the beatings she miscarried four babies, one

after the other. After her father died she asked her mother if she could come home, and her mother agreed on condition that she left Charlie Martin behind in Scotland. This was an easy condition, as by that time Charlie had left her, though her mother was unaware of that.

Shortly after she returned home her mother also became ill. She, too, had to be looked after by a live-in nurse, for as Mrs Martin admitted to Megan, she herself couldn't boil an egg, let alone look after a sick woman. All these misfortunes had ruined the family, and now the bank foreclosed the mortgage on their house. She and her mother were reduced to living in a small, rented house on the hill, where her mother soon died.

Anyone could tell that Mrs Martin had known better things by the way she conducted herself, and the sort of things she had in the house. Moreover, she had always had to have a housemaid, even though she, and now Megan, knew she couldn't afford it. Everybody in the town believed Mrs Martin still had money because she kept a maid, which cost two shillings and sixpence a week. Indeed, Megan's sister Helen was her maid for a while before going to Belfast. Mrs Martin would cry when she was telling Megan about her past.

Although she had no money coming in, people would say, "Of course she's got money, how else is she living?" But only Megan knew how she was really living, because Megan was the one who would go looking for the same old Jew man who had bought all the family treasures from Helen. Mrs Martin would tell Megan, "Make sure he doesn't come to the front door." Every time the Jew man bought things for a pittance, Mrs Martin would cry, then send Megan over to Donoghoe's for a big jug of Guinness, or porter as it was then called. But she always told Megan she must say it was for someone else, never for Mrs Martin.

Poor girls from the town, who needed a reference so as to get work in England, would often ask Mrs Martin to write one for them, and Megan can see her now, sitting at her leather-topped desk, opening her lovely rosewood ink box, taking a pen and dipping it in the inkwell. Then she would write:

TO WHOM IT MAY CONCERN

I have known the bearer and her family for a good many years, and during that time I found her to be honest, trustworthy, and reliable. Therefore I have no hesitation in recommending her to anyone who may need her services.

Signed: Mary Martin

She would then read it through, seal the envelope and hand it over, saying, "Good Luck now, and may your God go with you."
When the girl had left, she would ask Megan, "Do I know that girl? Who is she, Megan?"
Then Megan would tell her all about the girl's true character, and that of her family. Even though she'd written hundreds of references for girls, she didn't know any of them.
People in the town wondered why Megan was still running messages now she was living with Mrs Martin. But Megan promised her that she wouldn't tell anyone about the old Jew man, or indeed about her drinking. Megan would tell the old Jew man not to come before 3.30pm, because by then the maid would have gone home, but she often wondered what the maid thought when she'd come in next day and things would be missing. She would probably not have noticed at the beginning, when it was just personal items, but then her writing-desk went, along with her grandfather clock and other big items. The Jew man used exactly the same approach over the grandfather clock as he had over Helen's jugs. He didn't let up, until he had got what he was really after – and yes, he got the clock for a pittance.
Sometimes Mrs Martin would sit reading her brother Charles's medical books and would pencil around paragraphs. When Megan asked her why she was doing this she said, "It's because I don't feel very well and I want to find out why I am in so much pain." She went on to tell Megan that that was why she was drinking, to kill the pain. Megan asked her why she didn't go to Doctor McCann, 'the rich man's doctor,' as she was called.

Doctor McCann was never known to see to the poor, nor would the poor dare to approach her. Doctor McCann's husband was the only solicitor in town, they used to walk up the hill together in their fine clothes, neither looking or speaking to any of the poor of the town, though they were happy to play tennis with the priests, the bankers and the Cosgroves. Their only daughter, Margot, was boarding at Lorretta Convent, Dublin, but when she was home for the holidays, she also wasn't encouraged to speak to poor kids from the town. Indeed, when she and her family walked up the hill, the poor kids would stand aside to let them pass.

"Should I go and get Doctor McCann?" Megan asked. "She speaks to you, doesn't she?"

"Yes, she does speak to me, but I do not want you to get her. I haven't the money now, and I don't want her to know that."

Megan would watch her gripping her body with pain, for the drink no longer seemed to help, and although Megan knew nothing about periods or indeed cancer, she wondered why Mrs Martin's clothes were always bloody and smelly. She would ask Megan if she could take them away and dump them somewhere, as there were no bins in those days.

Megan was at a loss to know what to do with the smelly, bloody pile of clothes, so she decided to ask Mrs Gaffney, who lived opposite, for advice. "Bring them over here, I'll burn them in the back garden," she said, but when she saw the state of the clothes, she went over to see Mrs Martin, and when she saw how bad she looked, she said, "I'm going to get the doctor, you cannot go on like this."

"What Doctor are you going to get?" Mrs Martin asked.

"Well any, who do you want? Mrs McCann, isn't she the family doctor, wasn't it her who used to see to your mother and father?"

"Well, yes, but I cannot have her any more."

"Oh go on with you, she'll see you!" Mrs Gaffney then wrote a note for Megan to take to Doctor McCann.

"I would like you to give this note to Mrs McCann," Megan

said when the maid opened the door, "it's from Mrs Martin."

"Oh, alright, I'll give it to her when she comes back from Dublin tonight."

"She's in Dublin, she'll be back tonight," Megan told Mrs Gaffney. "Right then, you and me are going to help get her into bed. It's a wonder she's been able to stand up."

"No, I don't want to go to bed, I'll sit here, I can't rest with this pain, I'll only get out again."

Mrs Gaffney liked Mrs Martin, as everybody did, because of her kindness to the poor, whilst she still had money. Mrs Gaffney also knew she had been drinking to try to kill the pain, so she said, "I'll go across and get you a drop of whiskey. Come, Megan, I'll give it to you."

In Gaffney's, Mrs Gaffney told Megan she thought that Mrs Martin was riddled with cancer. "She knows she's dying, Megan, and she asked me to make sure that you have that nice feather bed and all the bedding."

"What will happen, Mrs Gaffney?"

"Oh, she knows she's not going to make it."

"So she – Doctor McCann – will probably send her to the workhouse!" Megan cried. "My God, she's always had a fear of ending up in there! She's always saying she would rather die on her feet than end up in the workhouse."

"It's sad, Megan, for someone like her to end up in a place like that, but I'm afraid that's what it's going to be. You know and I know, she has nowhere else to go. It's very sad, Megan, but then life is very cruel sometimes."

Doctor McCann came on Thursday night, and Mrs Martin was taken away Friday morning. Once again Megan boarded Donnelly's bus the following Monday; she was used to this journey by now, and now as before, Mr Donnelly wouldn't take her money. When she got there, a nurse greeted her with, "You must be Megan."

"Yes I am."

"Now we hope she'll go in peace, poor soul, she's been asking for you all weekend. She's very disturbed, something is bothering her, maybe you know what it is."

"Yes, I do know what it is," Megan said, and told the nurse the whole story of Mrs Martin's sad life.

"Come with me, now, and I'll show you where she is. Has she got no one else to visit her?"

"No," Megan, said, "just me."

Poor Mrs Martin looked terribly old. She was blind by now, but knew Megan was there. Almost shouting, the nurse said, "Megan is here to see you, isn't that nice? She's come over on the bus to see you."

As Megan gave her a kiss on the cheek, which the nurse had said she could do, she saw the tears roll down Mrs Martin's face.

"How long has she been sick?" the Nurse asked.

"Oh, a long while, but she wasn't in bed or anything like that."

"Well, now you have come, maybe she will settle down."

Mrs Martin died four days later, aged 54 years.

Mrs Gaffney hadn't fully realised how impoverished Mrs Martin had become, until she went with Megan into the house to get Megan's bed and to sort out what was left to be sold, so as to pay for the funeral. It was then she found the cheques that had been returned dishonoured by Mr Gilmore, manage of the Ulster Bank. "Do you know anything about these?" she asked Megan.

"Well not much, only she would sometimes send me with a letter to Mr Gilmore."

Mrs Gaffney, being the postman's wife, had probably thought that because Mrs Martin received letters from the Ulster Bank, she had money there, because no one on the hill had ever been inside a bank. So it was only when Mrs Gaffney was going through the papers that she discovered not only the returned cheques, but letters demanding money she owed. Mrs Gaffney told Megan that there was nothing she could do about Mr Gilmore and his Bank, but she was going to get someone to help her to get what was left in the house put outside and be sold. "An auction, yes an auction we will have. Go, Megan, and tell as many people as you can we are having a sale."

Tommy Flaherty and his young wife, Kathleen, who lived

next door, helped to carry out what was left, but when Kathleen saw how little there was, she too was shocked. Even she hadn't known how much the old Jew man had taken away.

After the sale Mrs Gaffney put all the takings into an envelope and sent Megan to take it to Mr Larry Kearnan and tell him that was all. Mr Kearnan owned the only hotel in the town, plus a big shop that sold everything from a needle to an anchor. He also made and sold coffins. His children also boarded at Lorretta Convent in Dublin and like the McCanns, made sure that when they were home for holidays they never mixed with or even spoke to the poor children of the town. Thus their only friend was Margot McCann, daughter of the rich man's doctor and the rich man's solicitor.

Years later Megan learnt that Larry Kearnan had a sister, Kitty Kearnan, who never came to the town. She had been mistress to Michael Collins. Michael Collins was Chief of the IRA from 1916 to 1918, and was shot, apparently by his own party. He is still remembered, and was recently the subject of a feature film.

After Mrs Martin's funeral Megan was back home, but not for long. Someone had told the local Canon, whose name was Kane, though he was no relation to Mrs Martin, about James beating Megan, so the Canon invited Megan to come to the Priest's House, which was a few hundred yards down the street.

"Hello, Megan," the housekeeper said as she beckoned her into a lovely cosy room with a big roaring turf fire.

Soon after the Canon came in to shake hands. "Sit down, Megan," he said, "the housekeeper will bring us some tea soon. I suppose you wonder why I have sent for you."

"Yes I do," she said.

"Well, it's like this, Megan. The Saint Vincent De Paul and myself have had a meeting, and we've decided that it would be in your best interest if you were sent to a convent in Navan." He went on to tell her why, and concluded, "I'll make the arrangements, and you will come and see me – one week from today, say – or I'll send you a message."

Megan left the Priests' House feeling devastated. She couldn't wait for Leonard to come home.

"Has he begod!" Leonard exclaimed when she told him, "Well, he's in for a shock. You'll be in Belfast before he knows you've gone."

Leonard told Nell Sheddock, another kindly neighbour who worked in Kearnans. She told Leonard, "Send a telegram to Helen and I'll give her the fare. Yes, me mother and me will pay her fare to Belfast."

So Megan was put on Donnelly's bus once more, this time to take her to Cavan. From there she'd get a train to Belfast, and Hell.

CHAPTER FIVE

When Helen met Megan at the Railway Station she looked ill and not at all pleased to see her. "I don't know what's wrong with me," Helen said, "I can't walk far, I'm tired all the time." Helen was very disturbed, and kept telling Megan she wouldn't like it there, which made her start to cry. That made Helen cry too. "I'm sorry, Megan, but I didn't know what I was coming to, but I had left school, so I got away as soon as I could. But you are only eleven, so you have a long way to go before you can get away, and GET AWAY YOU MUST."

Megan was devastated at Helen's welcome, but the ride was over.

"Here we are now," the tram conductor shouted, "Flax Street!"

"Come on, Megan, we still have a long walk yet," Helen told her.

Megan had been so excited at the thought of seeing Helen again, she broke down and cried, and again Helen cried too, but this time for Megan. "Megan," Helen went on to say, "this place and these people are not like what you've left behind. You knew everybody at home. You must always pray, yes, Megan, pray, that's what our father always told us and he would want me to tell you the same. Yes, pray, and if you are frightened ask Him to help you. God is always around us."

As they reached Ardoyne, Megan couldn't get over the never-ending rows and rows of houses. Then there were the unfamiliar air-raid shelters, and the back alleys. There were big men, all in black uniforms and helmets, walking up and down, up and down, carrying guns. They had long overcoats, big boots, and leather belts with holsters for their guns. "Don't keep looking at them, Megan, otherwise they will think we're up to something."

"What something?" Megan asked.

"Oh, I don't know," Helen replied, "you'll soon find out, and you'll get used to seeing these peelers on the street."

"What did you say, I thought you said they were called police?"

"Yes, I did say they were called police, like we used to call Garda's, same thing," Helen replied.

"But you just said 'peelers'."

"Well, that's the Belfast slang for police. Now, don't look at them again, and don't ask any more, you'll soon find out – yes indeed you'll soon find out."

And didn't she just! When they got to Brigit's house, the sister Megan never knew, there wasn't much of a welcome, no hug, or kiss; but by then Megan was used to not getting any affection, and had come to expect none. Megan was a bright, streetwise little girl, and she immediately sensed something not quite right in the atmosphere, but tried to ignore it. Brigit offered Helen tea, which she gave her in a big mug and the same to Megan, while they were still standing. As young as Megan was, she knew by looking at Brigit she was pregnant.

Four other children stood around, the oldest a boy about six, the youngest about 18 months, and on the right hand side of the fire sat a thin-faced man with fingers all yellow from chain-smoking, who had so far said not a word. Nor had he stood up, nor made any motion at all except to tap the ashes off his cigarettes and onto the floor.

"I'd better be going now," Helen said, but before she left Megan heard Brigit say to her, "You haven't got a few bob you could give me, having to keep her now and all that?" She was pointing at Megan as she spoke.

Helen gave her a half crown, saying, "That's all I can give you, I don't get paid until the end of the month." With that Helen said goodbye to Megan and left. The man still hadn't spoken a word to anyone.

"How's Leonard?" Brigit asked.

"He's alright, and James yes. He's alright too."

Megan waited for her to say something about Peter dying, but she asked after no one else. Megan remembered Leonard telling her about their father having red hair, and decided Brigit must take after him, as she too had red hair.

At this point the man got up and went upstairs. The four children remained ranged on the settee, looking Megan over. "Sit down," Brigit said, pointing to the chair the man had left, which was still warm. Megan sat down, looking nervously around. "Have you brought no clothes with ye?"

"Yes," Megan replied, pointing to the bag Helen had left on the floor by the door, "they're in that bag."

The silent man came back into the room, at this point. "Let Sammy have his chair now! Here, sit beside the children, move up, come on, move up, ye lot, let the wee girl sit down. What do you want for your tea, Sammy?" Brigit asked the man, "Shall I get you a few baps down the shop?"

Sammy replied, but Megan didn't understand a word. He lit another cigarette from the one still in his mouth, and carried on smoking. Brigit went into the kitchen, saying, "I'll go down and get a few baps and buns."

As she came out of the kitchen Megan noticed she was wearing a plaid shawl, like the gypsies wore when they came into her town on a Market Day, causing trouble and starting fights. The man still hadn't spoken to Megan, she was by now feeling terribly depressed and frightened to be so alone, thinking that from what Helen had said, she would be better off in the workhouse.

> *You cannot stop the birds of sorrow flying*
> *But don't let them build their nests in your heart.*

Brigit returned with the shopping in her hands, including milk in a bottle, not in a gallon jug. After a short while she shouted, "Come on ye lot!"

At that the children scrambled onto the floor to eat the round white bread rolls, called baps, and tea. Megan was given the same, but the butter tasted wrong. Megan didn't feel hungry, but tried to eat it. She wanted to cry, but remembered what Helen had told her: "God is always with you. When you are frightened, pray, Megan, pray."

Sammy handed his mug back, complaining that there wasn't enough sugar in it.

'Please God find me ten shillings to go back home to Leonard and James, even if James did give me black eyes.'

God did answer her prayers, but not for two and a half years.

Sammy put on his cap and his white scarf, and went out, still not saying a word, and leaving Megan to help Brigit put the children to bed. Their bedroom was very bare, containing one double bed and nothing else whatever. It had been shared by the three elder children, who must now make room for Megan as well. In the other room, which was almost as sparsely furnished with just a double bed and an old wardrobe, Brigit and Sammy slept with the youngest child.

Sammy had still not returned by the time Megan went to bed. She lay there crying silently and praying to God to help her get away from there, and was still awake when she heard shouting and banging downstairs, followed by the youngest child screaming. This woke the children lying beside her in the double bed.

"What's that shouting?" Megan asked the eldest.

"That's me Da, he comes in drunk and they fight. He's a Prod, and me Ma and us are Fenians."

"What's Prods and Fenians?" Megan asked.

"Fenians are what Catholics are called and Prods are Protestants, and me Da's a Prod, but they'll be alright tomorrow," the child continued.

"Has Daddy got a job, I mean does he work?"

"Yes, he runs messages for a bookie in the middle of the City. Me Ma and us meet him there sometimes and he gives me Ma some money. Me Ma likes to go and get the money before he spends it on drink."

As the children had predicted to Megan, they were 'alright tomorrow'. Indeed, one wouldn't believe the rows of the night before, when you saw the pair tucked up in bed together. Megan saw this as she made her way into the bathroom, so that she could try and get dressed without the children seeing her all wet and pee'd upon. It was quite late and there was no movement from Brigit and Sammy's room. She made her way downstairs, followed by the children, half naked in the grey-coloured vests they had slept in, wet halfway up their backs with urine. The old nightdress that Megan had taken off was just as wet. She wasn't sure which of them wet the bed, maybe all of them.

The older boy told Megan, "Me Ma and me Da likes a mug of tea in bed, with a fresh bap." It was his job to get the bap from the little shop at the top of the road, using money that he got from his Da's pocket.

Whilst the boy was away for the baps Megan made the tea, and washed the mugs that were still lying in the sink from the night before. By the time he returned, Megan had found out where things were kept in the small kitchen, and the little girl, who said she was nearly five, told Megan, "Me Da has the butter on his baps and we have the margarine."

Now Megan realised why the butter hadn't tasted very nice last night. The little girl went on to tell Megan that she talked funny – "You talk just like Helen did, and me Da used to make fun of her."

"Don't you go to school?" Megan asked.

"Yes we do, but not today, 'cos you're here. We go to the Holy Cross School on Crumlin Road. Me Ma says you might go to the Convent, that's down the Crumlin Road. The Convent is next door to the Crumlin Road Jail and the Mater Hospital. The two wee girls down the road go there. But me Ma says you might not go to school if you don't want to."

Megan thought it was the child who 'talked funny', but was too frightened to say so in case she told her Da. Megan now realises just what is best defined as human scum. Sammy serves her as its archetype.

"What's your brother's name, the one that's gone to the Shop?"

"That's Peter, but we call him Pete," and pointing to the other child, "He's Sam. He's called after me Da." (God help him,

Megan thought to herself.) "And my name is Louie, and the one with me Ma and Da is Dan."

Pete now returned with these things called baps, and another bottle of milk. "You didn't take the empty bottle back," the little girl shouted.

"Oh, it don't matter."

"Do you always get your milk in a bottle?" Megan asked.

"Course we do, what ya think we get it in?" asked Peter.

"Well, where I come from we get it in a can or jug."

They all laughed at this, which made Megan want to start crying again, but instead she prayed silently.

'Sacred Heart of Jesus, I Place all my trust in you,
Immaculate, Heart of Mary Help me.'

Pete took one mug of tea upstairs and came back for the other, Megan following him with the baps. She waited outside the bedroom door for Pete to take them in, and while she was waiting, glanced through the opening of the door. There was Brigit sitting up in bed alongside Sammy, who was smoking and sipping his mug of tea. After their so-called breakfast of baps and margarine, Megan helped the children to put on their clothes, which were still lying where they had dropped them the night before. They got dressed on top of their wet vests and unwashed legs.

The big men in black were still walking up and down, up and down, carrying their guns. Megan opened the back door and looked down the steps into the little yard. It was surrounded by a wall, with a door leading out to a great long alley, strewn with every kind of rubbish, including dead animals. Even so there were children walking through it on the way to school.

It was some time before the two upstairs appeared, first Brigit, who lit the fire, then, about mid-day, Sammy came bouncing down on the lino stairs. Brigit was acting as if nothing had happened the night before and Sammy took his place by the fire. Megan couldn't bear to look at him, nor did he look at or speak to her.

It was only when Brigit told Megan that she was going to Lipton's on Crumlin Road, and that she was taking her with her to carry the bag, that Megan noticed the mouthful of yellow teeth Sammy had, to match his yellow fingers. Even when Brigit asked him for some money, he kept the fag in his mouth whilst he counted out the small change. Brigit handed Megan the bag, whilst she put her hideous plaid shawl back on, and with the baby in her arms they walked the long haul through Flax Street to the Crumlin Road.

Megan felt like a child in solitary confinement, not knowing who she was, or where she was, and with no one to turn to. She had known hard times, cold and hunger, but never felt so lonely, blank and useless as she did now. She glanced up at Brigit, wrapped in her tinker's shawl, and she wondered what Granddad would think of all this Belfast stuff, the Prod's, Fenians and Peelers. God what a dump, I'll never get used to this, she thought to herself.

"What ye crying for?" Brigit asked her.

"I want to go home."

"Ye have no home, that's why ye are here," Brigit shouted back. "You think yerself lucky that Sammy took ye in, back to the home ye were going."

As she said those things Megan wondered if Sammy made fun of Brigit talking, as she still had her Southern Irish accent.

"Yes, Mrs Levin?" the man in Liptons asked.

Handing over the ration books and smiling from ear to ear, she said, "I'll have all the rations today."

This is the first time Megan has seen Brigit smile, maybe it was because someone was being civil to her. Megan also noticed that although Brigit was quite young she had false teeth. Megan thought perhaps Sammy had knocked them out. Also that reminded Megan she hadn't cleaned her own teeth today, although she had brought a toothbrush with her, which she herself had bought with pennies from messages. She hadn't noticed any toothpaste in the scruffy bathroom nor did the other children seem to have toothbrushes.

When they returned from Liptons Sammy was still sitting smoking, with the ashes all around him. Megan could feel him watching her every move, and wondered how long before he would be going out to do whatever he did.

At last Megan smelt something frying and thought, God they do eat other things besides baps and buns, as they called cakes. Sammy was again handed his food first, a bap and a few sausages and a mug of tea. He continued to smoke while he ate. The children once again sat on the lino floor to eat their sausages. Brigit didn't seem to eat much, although she was pregnant.

After everyone was finished, Sammy pointed to the mug on the floor and said to Megan, "Take that out."

By now Megan had begun to realise that she had been brought there not out of love, but to serve as the family skivvy. She picked up all the children's mugs etc. and realised she was expected to wash them also. As she turned the hot tap on, Brigit turned it off, saying. "Don't use the hot water yet, the fire hasn't been lit long enough yet, and I want the water to get hot for washing clothes."

Meanwhile a lady came to talk about the baby Brigit was having. Megan heard Brigit tell the lady that she was going to be alright now that her young sister had come to help her. Brigit saw the lady looking at Megan, and went on to tell her, that Megan was very sensible, and that she has been looking after her brothers. At this point Sammy stood up and tied his white scarf round his neck. He put on his cap and, with the fag still hanging out of the side of his mouth, pushed off without saying a word to anyone.

By now it was late afternoon, and Brigit took Megan upstairs to help take the wet things off the bed. She then almost completely filled the bath with water, and shook in a whole packet of Rinso and half a bottle of bleach. All the wet smelly clothes went into the bath next, and she then took a washboard from behind the door and stood it in the bath as well. Finally, she told Megan that if she knelt down on the floor it would be easier on her back. As Megan did the washing she wasn't quite sure whether the strong bleach was making her eyes run more than the silent crying.

From then on, this was to be one of Megan's daily chores. Every Monday she went to Liptons for the rations, and every morning she was up first to get the two older children off to school. On her way back from school she would collect the baps, and the bottle of milk so as to serve Sammy and Brigit baps and tea in bed, where they would stay until mid-day. Meantime, Megan would clean out the grate, light the fire and do whatever else needed doing. If Sammy came down first, and Megan hadn't been able to get the fire going because the sticks were damp, she'd be frightened because he had taken to hitting her, and demanding what the f...ing hell was he keeping her for?

Brigit was no better; she expected Megan to wait up with her every night, however late, for Sammy to come home, and if Megan showed any sign of tiredness, her attitude was, "If I can stay awake so can you." So Megan took to going out to the kitchen and wetting her eyes, so as to stay awake. Brigit never failed to remind Megan how good it had been of Sammy to take her in to live there.

It was on one of those mornings when Megan couldn't get the fire started that the next-door neighbour heard her crying, and came around to find out why. The neighbour said she was going to report them both, as it wasn't the first time she had heard Megan cry, also that she ought to be going to school. The neighbour went on to ask, "How are you treating that wee girl, just like your other sister Helen, but she's only a child?"

Sammy told the neighbour to, "Mind her own f...ing business, you f...ing Fenian."

Brigit didn't come to the door to face the neighbour, nor did she speak to her ever again, but the neighbour did tell Megan in their hearing that she was to bang the wall the next time they hit her, and she would come around. A few days later a man from the School Board came to investigate why she wasn't attending school. Brigit told the School Board man that Megan was there on holiday and that she would be going back over the border, once she had her child, which was anytime now.

For a minute Megan thought what Brigit was saying was true, but of course, she had no intention of sending Megan back over the border after the child was born, nor indeed after the next one either. But she did go to school because the School Board man came back again. She was sent to a Sisters of Mercy convent on Crumlin Road, but by now she didn't care whether she went to school or not. Meanwhile she still had to get the other children out to school as well as herself.

The convent was about a mile and a half walk, if she didn't have the tram fare, which she often did not. There was no Irish language taught at this school, and the nuns were not so brutal as some in the South, but because Megan was from 'across the border', as they say in Belfast, she didn't aspirate the 'th' sound. Then the nun would get a twig off a tree, and say to Megan, "This is a tree. And this is a figure THREE." She would stand in front of Megan and say, "Watch my mouth: three, three, three." she would do this while the other children all laughed, until eventually Megan got it right, but that was far from being the end of her troubles.

Her twelfth birthday came and went, and no one knew or cared, not even Megan herself. She is now well and truly used to the sight of all the women wearing plaid shawls and carrying babies, and she is still doing the washing in the bath, now on Sundays after Mass. The fights went on as before, with their constant garnish of stale obscenity.

One day Brigit told Megan, "We have an aunt living in Belfast, our mother's sister." Megan was interested in this, hoping maybe to get away, but Brigit warned her that she too was married to a Prod, like herself. "But her husband isn't like Sammy, he's a bad lot, and hates Catholics, so stay away."

Megan presumed that was why they never saw her, but having a very retentive mind, she memorised the address. Megan was still most unhappy at the convent, although she didn't have to buy her own books any more. The nuns weren't especially cruel, nor indeed were the children, though children did tell Megan, "We know you don't go home at lunchtime, but sit in one of the lavatories eating your lunch." This of course was true, but she had thought no one knew. In fact Megan was ashamed to let anyone see her lunch of bread and margarine, which she made herself.

Another thing some of the school children did was when they were kneeling down saying their prayers, the children kneeling behind Megan would stick sharpened pencils into her feet where they showed through the holes in her shoes. Megan would laugh and pretend that she, too, thought it funny. Consequently they christened her 'The Comic Kid from the Irish Free State'.

Helen came to visit now and again, and Megan asked her once more if she would give her ten shillings so as to go back home. Helen told her she could not afford it, as she is saving to go to England to marry her English soldier. "Oh, can I come and live with you, Helen?"

"No you can't, not yet anyway. Philip will be going overseas, and I will be living with his parents until he returns from the war. At least this is what we think we're going to do."

Meanwhile, things don't change much in the Ardoyne, except Brigit's house was even more crowded, with more beds but no more rooms. Megan still woke up, with no idea of who had pee'd on her. Sammy still drank and shouted abusive remarks about the Pope to Brigit and Megan. Children still swung around the lamp posts in the street, and skipped to the tune of *'Somebody's stealing my butter, Please leave my butter alone, You can steal all my jam, my plum apple jam, But please leave my butter alone!'*

Of course Megan had no swinging around the lamp posts, nor skipping either, nor any little friend like Jayne Carters at home.

Brigit took all the children, including Megan, to watch the Twelfth of July Orange March pouring out of the Orange Hall on the Crumlin Road. Megan didn't know about those things, nor was she interested, but Brigit said she had to go to please Sammy. And on the same night Sammy will come singing, 'Sure, it's on the twelfth I love to wear the sash my father wore,' or 'King Billy crossed the Shankill but he'll never cross Ardoyne.'

Sammy was not only uncouth, coarse and ill-mannered, he was also illiterate. He would bring a News of the World home, and make Megan read the most sordid pieces out to him, at the same time making fun of her accent. Megan had come to loathe him, but never more than when he would clear his throat and spit into the fire, sometimes missing, leaving Megan to clean up after him. He had no self-respect, and consequently no respect for anything, or anybody – at least that is the impression he gave to Megan.

Another time, when Brigit had sent Megan to the chip shop in Alliance Avenue for a shilling's worth of chips, on the way back she encountered a crowd of B. Specials coming from a rifle range. They stopped her and said, "Come here, wee girl, where do you live?" and when she told them, they said, "Say that again!" When she repeated her address they started laughing and saying, "F... me, she's from the f...ing Free State." Then one of them lifted his foot and kicked the chips over her head.

When she got home and told Brigit how they were dressed she said, "You should have run when you saw those bloody B. Specials, you should know by now what they're like."

Up to then Megan hadn't met any, so she didn't know, but Sammy laughed, and told Megan, "Now they know who you are, next time, they'll break your f...ing neck."

"Is your face hurting?" the nun asked Megan one morning, "It looks swollen."

"Yes it does," Megan said.

"Come let me have a look."

When she saw it, the nun said, "I think you should go next door to the Mater Hospital and let someone see you."

When the doctor saw Megan he said, "You have mumps, you shouldn't be in school, now go home."

Brigit was glad to see her, but instead of offering her any comfort, she just set Megan to her chores, one which was to wash Sammy's feet, which he was soaking in a bowl of water. She had done this many times before, whilst Sammy sat smoking and blowing smoke into her face. Brigit would say she couldn't bend down because of her big stomach. The hard skin on Sammy's feet was like boards and Megan would try to pull it off. That was the only time Megan ever saw him change his socks, and then they would be new socks. The socks he had been wearing would be thrown out, because by now they too were so hard they could stand up by themselves, without the help of his feet. The chore recurred every few months and Megan found it very unpleasant, but this particular day was worse, as she had to bend down with her sore face. The pain was atrocious, but she didn't cry any more, nor did she get any kind of treatment. She got moaned at, however, because now she would give the mumps to everybody else in the house.

When Megan returned to school the same nun asked her about getting confirmed, and went on to say that if she hadn't got a white dress she could borrow one. Children who had made their Confirmation would give their dresses to the nuns if they no longer needed them. When Megan told Brigit what the nun had said about borrowing a dress, she said straight away, "Tell her yes, you will borrow a dress, and shoes too. There's no one here who can buy you white shoes."

But Megan didn't ask for shoes, so Brigit bought her a pair of white plimsolls. Megan was the only child wearing plimsolls to her Confirmation. The school had laid on some bits of food afterwards for the children and the parents, but Megan couldn't stay because the woman whom Brigit had asked to be Megan's sponsor was herself pregnant and had to get back to the rest of her own children. Confirmation to Megan was just like any other day. There was no going into other children's houses, showing off your nice dress, and getting money from various people, which is how she remembered it was for children in the South after First Communion and Confirmation.

A few days after her Confirmation, Megan asked Brigit where the dress was, as the nun had asked for it back. Brigit kept making excuses for not being able to produce it. Then, when Megan finally, said "I have to bring that dress back on Monday," Brigit told her the truth.

"I haven't got the money to get it out of the pawn."

When Megan heard her say that, she remembered what Brigit used to say about the three balls outside a pawnshop – two balls to one you don't get it back.

> *I'm so lonely sometimes*
> *It's like walking down the street*
> *And the sound of my own footsteps frightens me.*

It was under the impetus of this crowning shame that Megan made up her mind to run away. On the next Sunday morning, instead of going to Mass, she walked from one end of Belfast to the other in search of Helen. All she knew was that Helen worked and lived in Ashley College, somewhere on Malone Road. After a long time, exhausted, cold and hungry, she found it. As she waited, having rung the bell, Megan glanced around at the lovely gardens. Such peaceful surroundings, she thought, not like Ardoyne at all. The only sound she could hear was the birds, and for a few moments she could have thought she was in a different world.

The door was opened by a young girl of about twenty. "I've come to see my sister Helen," Megan said.

"Oh, do come in, I'll get her for you."

Megan waited in the big hall until Helen appeared, looking very worried, and when Megan told her she had run away and wasn't going back, Helen replied, "I don't know what I'm going to do with you, I only work here myself."

Megan asked if she could have a drink of water.

"Yes, wait here. I'll talk to the other girls, whilst I'm getting you a drink."

> *At last dear Lord I'm free*
> *And I trust you'll walk with me.*

The young girl who had opened the door came back and beckoned Megan to come through. As she entered the great, warm kitchen all five girls welcomed Megan, pushing food in front of her. Whilst eating and crying Megan heard the girls discussing what and how they could help. They reached a conclusion as to what Helen should do, but not before Megan had asked Helen once more for ten shillings so that she could go back home.

Helen refused because she would be sent back to the convent, if she did.

Between tears Megan said, "I'd rather go back to the convent than back to Brigit's and Ardoyne and those six kids." This was even though Megan had come to love the children; and indeed they were nice children. Even more than Brigit's entire environment and lifestyle, it was her total lack of standards which revolted her.

The other servant girls at the college, of whom two were from Derry and two from County Tyrone, decided that Megan should be hidden in Helen's room until Helen's next half day, which was on Thursday, four days ahead. Then Helen would take her to a domestic agency, and pay the fee of five shillings, to which they contributed one shilling each. Meanwhile the girls would sneak food to Megan, telling her to make no noise, and not to open the door to anyone other than themselves. They told her what day the Housekeeper made her inspection, and that if she should go into Helen's room, Megan must hide under the bed.

On the Thursday Helen wasn't too sure what to do with Megan. She finally decided she would take her to see the aunt whom Megan had only heard Brigit talk about, and who lived on the Shankhill Road. Her aunt wasn't a bit like Brigit's description, and she cried when she heard Megan's story. Megan was her dead sister's child, but even so she was unable to be of help, as she had her own family, and she herself was married to a Protestant and living on the Shankhill Road. "It just wouldn't work," she told Helen sorrowfully, and added that she must either send Megan back home or take her to an agency as originally agreed. "You'll have to say she's fourteen, which she will be in a few months' time anyway."

Helen and Megan left for the agency where they paid her money and were given the address of an hotel down by Belfast Docks where there was a vacancy for a kitchen maid. The wages were two pounds per month, and the hours six days per week from 6.00am to 4.30pm.

Megan was delighted to get the job, but was worried when

Miss Beckett, the housekeeper said, "You don't look old enough, and it's very hard work."

"Oh, she's used to hard work," Helen replied. "She's been in a house full of children," she added, without letting on whose house it was.

"Right then," the housekeeper said, "I'll show you where you'll work, and where you'll sleep. You'll share a bedroom with the cook that you'll be working with. Sally, yes Sally's her name."

The bedroom had two single beds, divided by a thin partition, and down the corridor on the left there was a bathroom. Before Helen left, the housekeeper asked her where she could get in touch with her, should it be necessary. Helen gave her the telephone number of the college, and with that she left, saying that she was waiting for her passport to go to England.

The housekeeper showed Megan the big kitchen where she was to work, and told her that Sally would bring her down in the mornings. There was no mention of food, then or for the rest of the day, so Megan went back hungry to her room where she unpacked the two brown paper bags she had brought with her, and which contained such few bits of clothing as she possessed – gifts from the girls and Helen. Having packed them away in one of the drawers, there was nothing left but to sit down on the bed, cry a little, and say her prayers.

> *We are all Prisoners of our past*
> *You can never escape from it*
> *However much you try.*

Next morning, Megan was awake long before the person on the other side of the partition stirred. Although Megan had heard her come in during the night, she hadn't seen her because her bed was behind the door. Megan had also thought she had heard voices, but dismissed that thought from her mind.

Megan got dressed quietly and sat on the bed, not knowing what time it was, as she had been in bed since the previous afternoon. So she was well and truly rested and eager to get moving, but very hungry. She sat there in silence for what seemed a very long time until she heard a groan from the other side of the partition and a voice that said, "Are you there, wee girl?"

"Yes," Megan said, jumping to attention, pleased that at last there were signs of life from the other side. Looking round the partition, Megan saw Sally lying on the bed, fully clothed apart from her shoes. She looked about thirty-five years old, her dyed blonde hair was standing on end, and all her make-up was still on, including copious black eye-shadow. "Away downstairs with ye," Sally told Megan, "I'll be down shortly."

"Alright," Megan replied, not remembering where the kitchen was. But it must be down, she thought. She met a man in uniform, who showed her where the kitchen was.

Sally arrived, looking cross and bedraggled. "What age are ye, wee girl?"

"Fourteen," Megan replied.

"You don't look fourteen to me, when were you fourteen?"

"Six months ago."

"What month was that?"

Megan had to think quick. "December."

"What School did ye go to? You haven't got a Belfast accent."

That question told Megan that Sally was probing her to find if she was Fenian or Prod. They always ask what school you went to, not what religion you are. "I went to the Convent on Crumlin Road."

"So, you're a Fenian then."

"Yes, I believe that's what we're called," Megan replied. Though young, Megan learnt fast.

Sally didn't take her eyes off her. Looking her up and down, she carried on her interrogation. "So, you're from the Free State, the way you talk."

"I suppose I am."

"So why were you going to School here?"

"Oh, it's a long story," Megan replied, "but my parents are both dead, and I came here to live with a relative."

With her eyes still boring into Megan, Sally pointed to a sack by the great metal sink. "You can start peeling them spuds there."

"How many do you want peeled?"

"Fill those big pots, and then when you've done that, after breakfast do them cabbages there."

While Megan stood at the sink, staff were coming and going with trays and trolleys. They mainly looked at Megan and nodded without speaking. Presently Sally said, "It's nearly eight o'clock now, set that table for the girls. There'll be eight altogether."

Megan could see the open box of cutlery. "Do I put a tablecloth on?"

"No, don't bother about that, just milk, sugar, salt and pepper and the bread."

By now a few girls were sitting down. "Here," Sally said, "take these over to the table." On the plates were an egg and two sausages each. "No one wants porridge again, I suppose?" There was a ragged chorus of 'no, thankyous'. "How about you, wee girl?" Sally still hadn't got round to asking Megan her name.

"Yes please, I'll have porridge."

"Well, help yourself," she offered, pointing to the big, black stove and a pot that Megan could hardly reach.

Megan noticed Sally didn't sit down herself, but carried on working at the big stoves, now and again sipping from her teacup, between drags on her fag.

"What's your name?" one of the girls asked, "You're not very old ... how old are you?"

Again Megan said she was fourteen.

"So this must be your first job?"

"Well, yes, but I've done housework before in my sister's."

"You're not from Belfast are you?"

All eyes were now turned on Megan, wanting to know why she was already living in at only fourteen. "What does your parents think of you being away from home so young?"

"Oh, they're dead."

After that conversation stopped, and the girls were less inquisitive.

By four o'clock Megan was on her knees, but at least she

could go to bed. She was so tired, she thought she would only wash her feet that were so sweaty and dirty, but when she noticed how dirty her knees were from kneeling, she decided to have a bath. During her few years with Brigit, Megan had done a lot of thinking, and now it was paying off. For when she decided to make a run for it, she knew from her visits to Liptons, that everyone should have a ration book and clothing coupons. Therefore, before she left she had taken her own ration book and some clothing coupons to which she felt she was entitled.

When she came into the hotel the housekeeper hadn't mentioned her ration book, so before she went to bed she decided to go back down to find the housekeeper to give it to her. Megan couldn't find her office so she thought she'd wait until she asked for it, as she did later. When she returned to the bedroom Sally was there, lying on her bed. "I thought you had gone out, wee girl," she said.

"Oh, I won't be going out, I've got nowhere to go to. I'd go and see my sister Helen, but she forgot to give me the tram fare, besides she's a domestic servant, and won't be free. It doesn't matter anyway, she's going to England in a few weeks' time, when she gets her passport."

Sally was nodding off, so Megan stopped talking and got into bed, only to hear Sally start snoring. As she lay there listening to Sally's snores, Megan wondered if Brigit would come looking for her. But when she sees I've taken my ration book she'll know I'm not coming back, and that's good. Eventually Megan fell asleep, and it was very dark when she was awakened by the noise Sally was making opening drawers and pulling them out. "Oh, is it time to get up Sally, am I late?"

"No," Sally said without looking at Megan, "It's 9 o'clock at night."

Megan tried looking at Sally without seeming to. I suppose Sally reckons she looks great, Megan thought to herself, with her bleached hair all piled on top, and all that make-up, her high heels, and leopard-skin coat and that fag in her mouth, God, those people and their fags!

As she was leaving Sally told Megan that when she locked the door to the room, she must always take the key out, otherwise Sally wouldn't be able to get back in, so as soon as she'd gone, Megan did lock the door and took the key out. She would have locked the door anyway, because she had began to think that it might not be all that respectable a hotel.

The corridors weren't very nice, quite scruffy some might say, and she was nervous. Even when she went to the bathroom she didn't like the look of some of the men walking along the corridors. Also, when she thought she would open the windows to let the smoke out, all she could see was water and ships. It was very frightening, and she soon shut the window.

Megan did go to sleep again, but was woken when Sally came home, bringing someone with her. As Megan lay there she thought perhaps Sally was hiding someone, as Helen had hidden her, yes hiding someone under the bed. But whoever it was left later, and Sally went back to bed and snored and snored.

Megan was up and ready early next morning, but she crept around quietly in case Sally scolded her. She wasn't sure what to do, as she didn't know what time it was. Then she thought Sally might have left her watch on the chair beside her bed, and thought she'd have a look. Sally was lying partly clothed lying on the bed with her watch on her wrist, but Megan was too scared to look and decided that as she was dressed she would go and try to find out what time it was elsewhere. She wandered around for ages before she saw anyone, then a man who said he was a night porter asked her who and where she was looking for.

She told him who she was, and that she wanted to know the time, "Oh, you shouldn't be wandering round here, wee girl, it's not safe. Go on back and I'll knock on your door at 5.30. It's only 4.00am now. From then on the night porter would knock every morning.

The routine in the kitchen went on much the same, only Megan got to know the other girls. Some were chambermaids, which was a much easier job than kitchen maid, and Megan wished she had such a job. One girl called Clare was from Lurgan, the others were from Dundalk and Derry and all around the South. On Sundays Megan washed her few things in her bath water and hung them over the bath until most of the water was out. Then she hung them on a piece of string she had brought from the kitchen, which she strung between the window-latch and a nail on the bedroom partition. Sally was always absent all day on Sundays.

Megan assumed she must have relatives in Belfast, and wondered how old she actually was. Sally certainly looked older than Brigit, but it was hard to tell. She could be thirty-five or forty. Megan didn't talk much to Sally, because she wasn't sure Sally liked her, and because when Megan did say anything, Sally never looked at her when she replied. At other times Sally would stare at her from top to bottom, in a way that made Megan uncomfortable.

After two weeks, still no one had been to see her, and Megan hadn't left the bedroom except to go to the kitchen and of course the bathroom. The other girls bought her some comics to read on Sundays, and when she wasn't doing that, she looked out the window, watching the sailors coming and going and of course watching the ships. By now she had seen HMS Trumpeter, HMS Pegasus, and HMS Vancouver and wished she was going away on one of them. She collected whatever food she could from the kitchens on Saturdays, and put it in her drawer. Her water she got from the bathroom. That was her Sunday food, as the kitchen was locked on Sundays and everyone seemed to be out except Megan – at least, so she assumed, as she saw no one. She'd discovered that there was another, smaller kitchen for light meals, but she had no money.

Megan assumed that was why she never saw the other girls after four o'clock, they must be working in the still room.

Megan hated the long, lonely Sundays, and tried to stay in bed with the covers over her head until Sally went out. On weekdays she could go back down to the kitchen about 4.30pm, when Sally was taking her nap to refresh herself for the night's activities. Then she would prepare vegetables ready for the next day, so as to get Sally off her back. Sally was always in a bad mood in the mornings, and shouted at Megan to "move yourself, wee girl," and this idea had made for a more peaceful life – so far anyway. But with the kitchen locked on Sundays, Megan couldn't get in to get ready for Monday morning, and this worried her. Sally was always looking for an excuse to have a go at her, so she avoided her as much as possible, until one night Megan forgot to take the key out of the bedroom door. Sally, coming back much the worse for drink, couldn't get her key in and banged on the door so hard she disturbed other members of staff, who saw how drunk she was.

When Megan finally woke and ran to let her in, Sally didn't give her the chance to say how sorry she was for forgetting to take the key out – she just grabbed her by the hair and set to beating her about the face, and cursing her for a "f...ing Fenian."

Megan put her hands up to protect her face, and she thought she had done so until next afternoon when she went down to the kitchen as usual at 4.30. The housekeeper and manager came on their rounds, and asked Megan why she was still there. She said she didn't mind as it left it a bit easier for her the next day. The housekeeper went on to ask her why she had a bruised face and arms. Megan made some excuse, but the housekeeper wasn't having any of it, and told Megan to dry her hands and come to her office. Probably someone had reported Sally, as the inspection was suspiciously well timed.

The housekeeper, who had written down Helen's phone number at work, said, "I'm calling your sister to ask her to come and take you away. This job is too hard for you."

"Oh, but I'm doing it alright, don't you think I am? Please don't send me away, please!"

"No, I'm sorry, I cannot employ you here any longer, otherwise, I may get into trouble myself. Besides, I think the work is too hard for you."

Megan listened as she spoke to Helen, and was worried about what Helen would say once again. "Your sister will collect you tomorrow. You've been here three weeks now, but I will pay you for four. I think a job with children would suit you better," she continued, "Would you like me to ring the agency I got you from, and see what they have to offer?"

"Yes, alright," Megan replied.

"Well, you just wait outside, whilst I ring around."

Later she called Megan in to tell her that she'd got her somewhere, on the outskirts of Belfast, a place called Balmoral, with a Mrs Mercer. "She's looking for someone to help look after her two-year-old, and she's expecting another baby."

Megan didn't really want to look after children, not after Brigit's six, but as she sat in the office she had no real choice. The housekeeper asked Megan a lot about herself before asking, "Does Sally come in late, and is she alone, and is she drunk? It's alright to tell me now, don't be afraid. I'll put you in another room tonight, so as you don't see her. Is that why you didn't tell anyone, because you're frightened of Sally?"

"Well, yes, besides I wanted the job."

"You mean, you needed somewhere to live, isn't that more like it?"

"Well, yes I suppose it is." With that Megan broke down and cried, and cried.

"You should have told me before what Sally was doing to you."

"I couldn't!"

"Why couldn't you?"

"Because, because ..."

"Yes, go on, Megan."

"She used to push my head out of the window so as I could see the docks, telling me, 'see them docks, I'll get some sailor to dump you in there, and you'll never be missed, you have no one to come looking for you.'"

"Did you believe she'd do that to you?"

"Yes I did."

The housekeeper then took Megan upstairs to her room, to collect her few belongings. Megan opened the door quietly so as not to wake Sally, who was lying on her bed in her working clothes, snoring. The housekeeper took one glance at her, then looked back at Megan.

That night Megan slept in a makeshift bed in Clare and

Rosalind's room. The next morning the girls told Megan to stay in the room until they had found out what Sally had to say. But shortly after eight o'clock, Clare came and told Megan to come and have something to eat, and that Sally was leaving that morning, thrown out, "Yes, thrown out!" Clare went on to say that the housekeeper had waited up for Sally the previous night, and that because Sally had thought Megan had been moved to another room, she had brought a sailor back, up the back stairs, "Yes, and both very drunk."

Clare said that Miss Beckett had asked the night porter to watch and see if Sally was drunk, and to ring her when Sally came home. The housekeeper then went to Sally's room, and found her with the sailor. The night porter threw the sailor out, and Miss Beckett told Sally to be out by next morning.

CHAPTER SIX

When Helen arrived to collect her, Miss Beckett handed Megan her ration book plus her monthly wage of two pounds and the address of her new employer, Mrs Mercer. Miss Beckett then wished Megan good luck and they left.

"Have you got your clothes coupons?" Helen asked as they walked out.

"I think so," Megan replied.

"Well, we had better go to Littlewoods and get you a few bits of underwear and things before you go to this Mrs Mercer, or whatever she's called. Balmoral is a long way out," Helen went on, as she impressed on Megan the need to get settled before she left for England. "You must stick this place," she said, ignoring the bruises on Megan's face, let alone what she had on her arms and body, which were covered by the old, faded coat that Helen had given her earlier.

Megan did stick it with Mrs Mercer, but only until Helen had left for England. Before going, she reminded Megan that if anyone asked her how old she was, she must remember to say she was fourteen, "because when I'm gone you could be put into a home in Belfast."

As Helen said this, Megan thought anything would be better than Brigit's. Helen went on to tell her, "Remember you must always pray, God is always around us, so you must call on Him at all times." She also promised Megan she would write and that she would send her a photo of her wedding. "Pray for me, Megan, and I will pray for you."

Megan was not to see Helen again for another four years.

Abandonment has been a
Central theme in my life
But when your own family do it
It's hard to take.

By the 1st of July, when Megan was fourteen in reality, Helen had been gone for several months. As she could now work without having to lie about her age, she thought she would look for something nearer Belfast city centre and her church, so once again she visited the agency in Donegal Pass. This time she was told of a Mr and Mrs Kennedy on Malone Road who were looking for a nursemaid. Although Megan wouldn't have chosen jobs looking after children, the agency didn't seem to want to offer her anything else, even though domestic servants were becoming harder to find.

The reason was that all the girls from across the border who were accustomed to doing domestic work in Belfast were now going to England to train as nurses. No Belfast girls were prepared to undertake domestic jobs, and called the domestic servants 'skivvies', which indeed they were. When you went for an interview you were never told what the hours were supposed to be; you would only be told what your wages would be, and which would be your half day off. It was taken as given that you would start about 7 am, and work until God alone knew. Very often it would be midnight before you would be told, "You can go to bed now."

There would be no time off for Bank Holidays, Christmas etc., nor was sick leave ever mentioned. Neither would anyone come to see if you were being overworked or cheated out of your wages – and of course, religion was never mentioned in those houses along Malone Road. Nonetheless, Megan had her interview with Mr and Mrs Kennedy, and decided to accept the position of nursemaid.

Megan still had to work her month's notice with Mrs Mercer, who told her one morning to hurry and get ready so as to go with her to Hollywood, a small town a few miles outside Belfast. There had been a bereavement in the family there, and they all had to go to London. Mrs Mercer's aunts wanted a member of the family to stay to look after the place whilst they were away. "And I need you to come with me to look after Patrick," Mrs Mercer concluded.

Megan had seen Mrs Mercer's aunts many times when they had come to visit, bringing gifts of all sorts of produce, such as baskets of fruit, vegetables, eggs and so forth. She always thought they must be wealthy, but nothing prepared her for what she was to see in Hollywood. Mrs Mercer had seemed very grand to Megan, but now she realised she was only a poor relation of the McCances.

There was a long private drive up to the big house, and when they finally got there the chauffeur opened the car door, just as the great door to the house swung open and the butler came forward to take Mrs Mercer's bag. Megan was left to fend for herself, which she didn't mind as she was used to such treatment. "Welcome, Madam," the housekeeper greeted Mrs Mercer, "you know where the drawing room is. The master and mistress are waiting for you, they are about to leave any minute now for London."

When the butler returned from taking Mrs Mercer's bags upstairs he said to Megan, "The housekeeper will show you your room in a minute, do take a seat, she won't be long."

Megan had never seen anything like that house before, or since. As she waited for the housekeeper to return she looked around at all the paintings of ships and more ships . The only time Megan had heard of the Titanic was when Brigit had told her that the reason the Titanic had sunk was because when it was being built by Harland and Wolffe, a Protestant workmen had written on it 'F... the Pope!' This legend exists in many forms, including the one where the Chief Engineer says, "God Himself couldn't sink this ship!" God then sets about proving him wrong, condemning nearly two thousand innocent people to a miserable death in the process. One wonders on exactly what sort of foundation some people base their faith.

There were no Catholics employed in the shipyards, Brigit said, because the money was good, and the Prods kept all the best jobs for themselves.

When the housekeeper returned she looked down where Megan's straw bag (given her by Mrs Mercer) lay on the floor, and asked, "Is this all you've got?"

"Yes, I'm afraid it is," Megan replied. "Mrs Mercer said we will only be here for a few days."

"Even so, it doesn't look much, however, come this way," she directed, leading Megan up the back stairs to the servants' quarters, which looked out over the farm labourers' cottages and greenhouses. "There you are, you have a nice view here, the bathroom is down the passage. When you're ready, come down to the kitchen for some refreshments."

"Yes, thank you, I will – thanks!" The kitchen was huge, warm, full of gleaming metal and awash with servants. She was asked her name, and everybody nodded their acceptance of her. "Sit yourself down, wee girl," the cook said. No sooner had Megan sat down, than a bell went, and looking at the bell board on the kitchen wall, the housekeeper said, "That will be for you, Megan, it's the drawing room. It's only your mistress that's in the drawing room now, so it's you she'll be wanting. Harriet, take Megan to the drawing room."

As they got to the top of the beautiful spiral staircase, Harriet noticed Megan looking down below. "That's the ballroom down there. We love it when they have a ball, we servants have a great time. Don't suppose we'll be having a ball for a long time now, with this bereavement ... There we are now," Harriet concluded as she knocked on the drawing room door, "see you later."

"Yes thank you, Harriet, thanks."

Megan loved it there. For the first time since she had been a baby, there was no housework; all meals were set in front of her, and she could eat as much as she liked; and in return, all she had to do was to push two-year-old Patrick around the grounds, pausing to chat with the people who worked on the estate. During one such chat one of the farm labourers' wives said, "You know that the master is in shipping of course, but we never see him. The master and mistress, Mr and Mrs McCance that is, are very nice to work for."

Megan told her, "Yes, I have met Mrs McCance many times when she has visited Mrs Mercer, her niece – that's my mistress in Belfast."

Megan returned to Balmoral after five days, sorry to leave Hollywood. Mrs Mercer had not, so far, interviewed anyone to be Megan's replacement.

CHAPTER SEVEN

The Kennedys lived in Adelaide Park, Malone Road. They had four children between them; Joan, aged fourteen, Patrick (yes, another Patrick!) about nine, Pamela about seven and a baby of about six months old. The three school-age children attended private schools, as did all children who lived on Malone Road. Megan's job was to help with the children, and Josie the housemaid did the rest. The first few weeks weren't too bad and Megan was pleased to be in walking distance of her church. Indeed, she could walk into Belfast city centre. Then one day Josie told Megan she too was leaving for England.

"You won't be wearing that nursemaid's outfit for long," she told Megan. "I started here as the nursemaid and ended up doing both until you came. They did have a housemaid when I started here, but then she left."

Josie was right, for when she left Megan was expected to do everything except the cooking. She would wear her nursemaid uniform to take Patrick and Pamela to school, then change into a housemaid uniform when she came home, and change again in the afternoon to collect them from school. No nursemaid on the Malone could be seen without a proper uniform, and there were no plaid shawls worn there. Nor did she see Peelers walking up and down, not once; nor did she hear the words 'Prod' or 'Fenian' used, nor indeed any mention of religion. Mr Kennedy being Head of Police, Megan was worried about being a Catholic, but religion was never mentioned, even when she asked for time off to go to Mass.

Mr Kennedy said, "Of course you can Megan, do you know where your church is?"

"Yes I do," she replied, and that ended the matter. Before Josie left, Megan would take her half day and go down to Lisburn Road children's playground, where she took the Kennedy children to play. She would stay there on the swings for a few hours, but would make sure she got back in time for tea. Normally she wasn't entitled to tea on her half day off, but if she got back in time to give the children their own tea, and clear up afterwards, Mrs Kennedy would then let her have some tea as well.

But now she was left to do everything, she got very tired and didn't take her half day off. Instead she did her few bits of washing, cleaned her room, washed her hair and took a bath. Then she fetched the children from school, said her prayers and got into bed early. That was the only night she could get to bed as early as ten o'clock.

Megan got to know a few people on the Malone Road from going back and forward to school, and being a chatty girl would often chat with them. One particular gentlemen, a very distinguished, classy-looking man, was now beginning to nod and raise his hat. He'd say, "You're early today, my dear," or "You're late today, my dear." He never seemed to be in a hurry, and soon began stopping for a chat, to and from Cadogan Park. He seemed to enjoy talking to Megan as much as she enjoyed seeing him, and asked her all about herself.

She told him everything, including Mrs Kennedy's having a job finding another maid, as no Belfast girls would do domestic work, and the girls from across the border were all going to England to train as nurses. "Is that so?" the gentlemen replied, "and will you be going to England one day to become a nurse?"

"Well, I will be going to England one day, but I'm not sure about becoming a nurse."

To that he replied with a smile, "Well I'm sure, my dear, whatever you do, you will do well. And one more thing, Megan," he said, "make sure you keep a diary, and one day it will keep you! Remember that," he said once more, before tipping his hat as he said goodbye. It wasn't until many years later that Megan learnt that joke had first been made by Mae West.

Work was getting very hard now in the Kennedy household, and Mrs Kennedy hadn't mentioned anything about giving Megan more money even though she was now working seven days a week. The only other people she got to talk to were the tradesmen, especially the postman. It was on one of those Saturday mornings when Megan was scrubbing the steps and polishing the brass, that the postman said, "You know, wee girl, when I've finished my rounds and go home, my children, some older than you, are still in bed. You worry me." He went on to tell Megan how Mr Flynn was saying how much he enjoys 'his little chats with you.'

"I don't know a Mr Flynn. I see a lot of friendly nice people on Malone Road, but I don't know their names. But there is one gentlemen I do stop and talk too, who I see turn into Cadogan Park."

"That's him, Professor Flynn, Errol Flynn's father."

"Well, I don't know his name."

"Everyone knows Professor Flynn! He sees you most days on his way to and from Queens University."

Megan hadn't a clue who Errol Flynn was either.

Listen and Learn
And Learn to Listen.

CHAPTER EIGHT

The postman kept his word when he told Megan he would keep any eye out for anyone who might want a maid, in a house without children, that is. It didn't take long, for with so many girls going off to England, Malone Road was finding it hard to replace them. "Look here," he said to her one morning, "I've got you a lovely place in Cadogan Park, just round the corner from here. An English family they are, no young children just one nineteen-year-old son at Queens, studying medicine. I've told the lady all about you, so go around on your next half day off – when is it? your half day I mean – so as I can tell her when you're coming."

"Well I haven't been taking any time off lately, I'm so tired, but alright then, Thursday, yes tell the lady Thursday about 4.00pm, well make it 4.30 in case I have to collect the children from school."

"Right," the postman said, handing Megan the lady's name and her number in Cadogan Park, "No doubt I'll see you before then to make sure you go."

"Oh, I'll go alright, I promise, and thanks, thanks again for your help."

"You're welcome, love."

Apart from going to Littlewoods once a month and the sweet shop to collect a few more bits of clothing along with her sweet ration, she had gone nowhere in the whole eight months she was with the Kennedys. On the Thursday of her appointment with Mr and Mrs Willis, Megan walked round the corner to Cadogan Park. She noticed the trees seeming to reach out to each other. Wouldn't it be lovely, she thought to herself, if only human beings could be like that. She rang the bell and waited for the big, heavy door to open.

"Good afternoon, can I help you?" the good-looking young man said in a lovely English accent.

"I have an appointment with Mrs Willis," she replied.

"You must be Megan then, do come in."

"Thank you."

"Take a seat in the drawing room," he said, pointing to a door opening off the great hallway, "I'll fetch my mother."

As she waited for what seemed ages, she looked at the grand piano which was open and had sheets of music scattered all over it. The room was cosy and warm with big, comfortable chairs and lots of cushions, plus a trolley laid out for afternoon tea. Just then the door opened and a very plain-looking lady came in with her hand extended, saying, "I'm sorry to have kept you waiting."

It was some months later that Mrs Willis told Megan why she had been kept waiting for so long, the reason being that when Tim, her son, went to get his mother they had argued about employing Megan. Tim had said to his mother, "You cannot possibly employ her, she's only a child!" Once again Megan was asked how old she was by a prospective employer, but she was able to tell Mrs Willis the truth this time when she said she had been fourteen since the first of July. Looking at this very plain lady, with no perfume, or pearls, or style, but very kind, caring and modest, her kindness almost made Megan cry. She hadn't received so much kindly interest since her dear friend Mrs Martin had died.

During the interview Mrs Willis said, "Frank, the postman that is, has told me all about you, but I didn't realise you were so young. However, if you've been looking after all those children and whatever, I'm sure you'll be fine here. Now let me show you around." Megan thought how lovely and quiet the house was, no screaming children, everything very orderly. She was also taken to meet Mr Willis in his study. He stood up to greet Megan with a handshake. Megan noticed Mr Willis was wearing a parson's collar, but she found out later that he was a psychiatrist as well as being a Presbyterian minister.

"I suppose you will have to give a month's notice," Mrs Willis went to on say, as she showed Megan into a large living-room-cum-kitchen with a large iron table with a cloth on it, running the full length of the room. Lifting the cloth, she said, "This is our air-raid shelter, which we use as a table for whatever." This room, Megan noticed, was also cosy and warm with a fire in the grate where the flames seemed to be saying, "You're welcome."

> *The quality of life*
> *Has a lot to do*
> *With the people you mix with.*

"Are you going back to Mrs Kennedy's now, and will you be able to get something to eat?" Mrs Willis asked her.

"Yes, I'll be alright as long as I get back in time to clear up, I'm allowed tea. Thank you anyway."

"Well, nice to have met you, Megan, and we'll see you in about four week's time. Perhaps you will let our postman know?"

"Yes I will, and it has been nice meeting you too, Mrs Willis."

As she walked back round the corner to the Kennedys, she didn't know whether to cry or not, she was so happy. But how was she going to tell Mrs Kennedy that she too was leaving? Megan wondered if she should bother to tell her at all, but then she thought if she didn't she would miss out on her month's money. And what about her ration book? Yes, my ration book, I must have that, she thought to herself. She did tell Mrs Kennedy, who offered to put her money up to two pounds ten shillings per month, but Megan stuck to her guns as Professor Flynn had told her to, thinking, 'Once I get out of here, I will never work in a house with children again, what with Brigit's and then this, no, no more children.'

After that the atmosphere in the Kennedy household became very cool, so Megan decided not to take any time off for the rest of her time there. Nor did she see anyone come for an interview. Mrs Kennedy and her fourteen-year-old daughter, Joan, were at one another's throats all the time.

It was during one of their arguments that Joan flounced out and went to her room, banging the door behind her. Mrs Kennedy told Megan to go and get her, and it was whilst Megan was talking to Joan, telling her that her mother the mistress wanted her down in the drawing room immediately, that Joan told Megan that, "'The mistress', as you call her, is not my mother." She went on to say that her own mother had died and daddy went on to marry her stepmother, whose own husband had been a pilot, but had been killed.

Megan had noticed that the other two children were much more like their mother, Mrs Kennedy. Joan confirmed this by saying that unlike herself they were her children and the new baby was Mr and Mrs Kennedy's. Joan went on to tell Megan that her stepmother would call her, look at Megan, and comment, "Look how Megan works, and she is only the same age as you."

CHAPTER NINE

The kindness Megan received from this English family was unbelievable. Even though she ate alone in the big kitchen, Mrs Willis would always make sure the fire was kept going. Things continued to be good, although she had a lot to do, and felt she earned her twelve shillings and sixpence a week, but the returns were good. Mrs Willis did all the cooking and was very good at it, and very organised, right down to planning her meals for the full week. She also did all her own shopping, except that the milkman and the baker delivered daily.

Breakfast was served in the breakfast room, where a fire had to be lit beforehand. The rest of the main meals were served in the dining room, where again a fire had to be lit every day. Afternoon tea was served in the drawing room and again a fire had to be lit, and kept going until bedtime. All those fires had to be cleaned out every day, as it was a large house with no central heating. The large dining-room table also served Tim and his friends from Queen's University as a pool table. Though the Willis household was by far the easiest Megan had served in, she still had plenty to do, from scrubbing doorsteps and cleaning brass to chopping wood and bringing in coal. She was up every morning at seven, but at least she was up to a lovely cooked breakfast. Whilst Megan might be setting the table in the breakfast room or wherever, she would very often come through to the kitchen to find her own table had been set by Mrs Willis, table napkin and all. Apart from the heavy cleaning Mrs Willis worked with Megan, from changing the beds including Megan's own bed, to washing, ironing etc. The coffee break every morning, which Megan had never had before, was always fresh ground coffee, one could smell it all over the house.

Never before or since had Megan known such a well organised woman as Mrs Willis, though she certainly wasn't an educated lady. In fact her son laughed at her because she couldn't spell X-ray. But what she didn't know about running a home wasn't worth knowing, and she kept an account of everything she spent, literally down to the last penny. Megan would see her after she returned from shopping, writing it all down in a notebook.

Mrs Willis insisted that all heavy work be done before 1.00pm. Then, after lunch, Megan would have to change into another uniform and continue with light duties. Meanwhile, on two afternoons a week, Mrs Willis set up her sewing machine on the air-raid shelter which was used as a table, to do her mending and making, which included her husband's suits, as well as Megan's uniforms. As she sewed she would be watching the clock, to see if it was time for afternoon tea. There was a day, an hour and a minute for everything in Mrs Willis' life.

Mr Willis always wore dark suits and black shoes, Megan noticed, and his two pairs of black shoes were identical. As soon as they bought a new pair, the first thing they would do is to have them soled and heeled before they even wore them. That way, Mrs Willis said, they would last longer. She would also tell Megan not to forget to change the shoes over every morning when she cleaned them, so that they didn't wear the same pair two days running.

Megan had never tasted Yorkshire pudding in her life before entering the Willis household, where Yorkshire pudding was always served with lovely onion gravy on its own. Saturdays were Mrs Willis' big cooking days, including a large pot of stockpot soup, with everything in it, enough soup to last the week, so everyone had soup first course every day. This was very economical, though I wonder what people would think of such an arrangement today, with the same pot being re-heated and allowed to cool seven times. Yet no one seemed to get food-poisoning, and Tim, the medical student, raised no complaint.

She would make everything from pies and puddings to cakes, and knew how many were in the tins from day to day. She was altogether a most remarkable woman, and of course, Megan's food was the same as the family's. When the gardener came twice a week she would set a place for him at Megan's table also, and he would tell Megan he had been looking forward to this meal all week.

The first week Megan was in the Willis household, Mrs Willis said to her, "You have one pot of jam per month. Now, you can eat it how you like, all in one go, but when it's gone it's gone. But what we, the family, do is, we share ours for baking etc., this way we all share the cakes and puddings etc., so what do you want to do with yours, Megan?"

"Oh, I'll do the same as you all do."

"Right," she said. "Then this way you will share in all the goodies."

One day when Mrs Willis was doing her sewing, Megan told her that her mother had been a seamstress. Mrs Willis replied, "Well, that was my trade before I married the master, and indeed after I got married I carried on at home, as the master was still at University and we needed the money." Then, looking up at Megan she said, "I don't think you've had your period yet, I would know if you had, you do know about those things don't you?"

"Well, only what Helen has told me, and no I haven't had a period yet."

"Well now," she said to Megan, "One should always be ready, so you see those squares I have cut and sewn?" pointing to some white material, "Get a needle and cotton from the sewing box and I will show you how to sew those loops on, those sanitary towels you buy are too expensive, so when the time comes you will have those ready, and I will show you where to keep a bucket of soapy salt water in the wash house outside so as to soak them until wash day. Then you'll wash them for next time." Handing Megan about two dozen of these squares she said, "When you have sewn the loops on, put them in your bedroom for when you need them, and, Megan, just in case of emergency, carry one if you should go out. Also take this piece of string until such time as you buy yourself a proper sanitary belt, you can get them from the chemist."

Mrs Willis went on to tell Megan that she, too, had come from a poor family. She had met the master when she attended his church back home in England. The master, she said, hadn't been much better off either. As well as being a minister, he had studied to become a psychiatrist, so she had to work at sewing to keep him at university. That was why she had only one child, and she was getting on when she had him. She would say, "You know, Megan, behind every successful man, there is a very strong, tired woman."

Megan got to know that Mrs Willis was not only a brilliant housekeeper, but a very fine lady where manners were concerned, and Mr Willis a fine gentleman. But Mrs Willis could never look like a lady, however she dressed. That's something you've either got or you haven't.

Megan's old Granddad used to say, "You can spot class, but you cannot describe it," and how true that is. Mrs Willis had a heart of gold, but no dress sense, but then again they say, fine feathers do not make fine birds. Mrs Kennedy and Mrs Mercer had class, and one could spot it straight away, but Megan admired Mrs Willis infinitely more for her kindness.

Mr and Mrs Willis would give Megan a lift to Mass on Sundays and would wait outside her church on their way back to pick her up. This would have never have happened in Ardoyne, but then, Mr and Mrs Willis were true Christians, they would have done that wherever they were.

They would also sometimes take Megan to the youth club attached to their church. She had never seen inside a youth club until then, and when the other children asked what school she went to, she said, "I haven't been to school in Belfast."

When Mrs Willis asked her why she had said that, she told Mrs Willis, "Well, here in Belfast when they want to know if you are Protestant or Catholic they ask what school you go to."

"Well, I never knew that," Mrs Willis replied.

"You wouldn't, would you? You live on Malone Road, and you are English."

Although she worked hand in hand with Mrs Willis, at night Megan always sat alone in her kitchen. She didn't mind, because they had put a wireless in there for her, and she could be heard singing along with it. They also made sure she kept her fire burning, and she could go to the study for books whenever she wanted. On Sunday nights after church, Mr and Mrs Willis would sometimes bring young English servicemen back for supper. When she knew she would be doing this she would tell Megan to light the oven half an hour or so before, so as to heat the lovely food that Mrs Willis had prepared earlier. There would also be a sing-song with Tim on the piano.

A Mr and Mrs Taylor who attended the same church, and who taught music in Dungannon, would also come. Mr Taylor, who was blind would always greet Megan as, "Our little Irish Colleen," and Megan loved those happy nights. Frank the postman still brought the mail, including letters from Helen, and he told Megan that Mrs Kennedy still hadn't got any maids and that Professor Flynn was pleased for her, and sent his regards.

Mr Willis thought that Megan ought to let someone know where she was, if only because of the bombing, and suggested she should trace her aunt at least. He was surprised Brigit hadn't reported her missing, but Megan was not, knowing that Brigit knew how much she hated it in Ardoyne. Besides Brigit couldn't care less what happened to her, now she was no longer doing her skivvying. "What about this aunt of yours, wouldn't she want to know?" he asked. Mr Willis, being English and living on the Malone Road, wouldn't understand why her aunt, being Catholic and married to an Orangeman, wouldn't be allowed to want to know about Megan.

"I'm alright really," Megan told them, "I'm doing fine. If you knew them you would understand, I have only seen my aunt once and she was worried then about knowing Helen and me, besides she has her own family to worry about." Mr Willis went on to argue that should they all be bombed, someone would have to be informed.

"Well, it won't matter then, will it? I'd rather be killed than go back to Ardoyne, I'm already nobody's child," she added, laughing as usual.

"So you don't know your aunt's name then?"

"No I don't, nor where she lives, no not really. All I know is when Helen and I went to see her, Helen asked the tram-driver to let us off at Sandy Row, but we didn't go down Sandy Row."

"What was her name before she was married – I mean your aunt?" Mr Willis went on to ask.

"Well, my Granddad's name was Fay, and she's his daughter."

Mr Willis, being a psychiatrist as well as a minister, would often have patients in his study, but when he had not he would often come down to the kitchen to have his coffee and a chat. He was always interested in Megan's past, and would laugh when Megan told him about Sammy's hard skin on his feet. She went on to tell him that Sammy would look as though he was walking on his heels because the soles of his feet were so bad, and Megan had to cut his toenails and try to scrape the hard skin off his feet. Laughing, Mr Willis said, "And did you have to kiss his feet afterwards?"

"No, but he thought I should, and so did Brigit."

Mr Willis came into the kitchen one morning for coffee and said he had traced Megan's aunt. "I have written to her," he said "and put our phone number on top of the letter, so don't be surprised if you get a call." To that Megan replied that she would be very surprised if she got a call, as it was only the elite who had phones in those days, and one could talk all day for two pence. Yet Megan's aunt did call, and Mr and Mrs Willis thought it right that they should invite her to visit Megan at their house, as Megan was frightened to visit her aunt on the Shankhill Road.

Being the lady and gentleman that they were, when Megan's aunt arrived Mrs Willis showed her into the drawing room, and bringing tea and biscuits in on a tray, told Megan not to hurry, that she herself would carry on with the chores. During the conversation she had with her aunt, Megan went on to tell her as much as she knew about her family in the Irish Free State, as she had now learned to call it. She told her aunt about her Granddad, who was her aunt's father, and how he was treated by her brother, Granddad's only son, and how he ended up dying in the workhouse, after Ben took off for Monaghan. This made her aunt cry, or at least she appeared to be sad. She went on to tell Megan that, being married with children and living on the Shankhill Road, and being a Catholic into the bargain, and trying not to let her neighbours know she was Catholic, she felt she had enough to worry about. Moreover, her husband being a bus-driver, there wasn't enough money to visit her father back home.

"Well, you look as though you have landed on your feet here, in this lovely big house. Have you heard from Helen? I don't suppose anyone else will ever hear from her, by that I mean there's no one here in Belfast she will want to know now she's in England."

"Yes, I do hear from her, and so do Leonard and James, but you are right when you say she's not interested in anyone else here in Belfast, she hated it like I do. I'm better off now that I'm here with this nice English family, but one day I'll be leaving Belfast myself. I have no fond memories of Belfast, at least that is until now. But however nice it is, it is still not like a family, and I am still a skivvy, but at least they are human, and indeed kind to me."

"So Brigit doesn't know where you are, does she?"

"Well no, nor do I want you to tell her either."

"No indeed, I won't tell her, besides I don't see much of her myself, only now and again on the Crumlin Road. And as for that drunk Sammy, he's a bad lot, was he still bashing that wee boy Pete?"

"Well, no more than he beat me," Megan replied.

"You know why he didn't like Pete? It's because he's not his child."

"Oh, I didn't know that, but I did notice that poor little Pete would make himself scarce when he was around. You could sense Sammy had no time for him, but who's his father then?"

"Oh, some bloke from the Falls Road, I believe, he took off when she told him she was in the family way, so she landed up in the Union."

"What's the Union?"

"Well, it's the same as the workhouse I suppose."

"God! Who took her out?"

"A woman who kept a doss house for men, and Sammy was one of the dossers."

"My God, you'd have thought she'd have learnt her lesson."

"She's well and truly in a no-return situation now, having all those children, and she's expecting again by the look of her. One every year so far," her aunt said. "Brigit doesn't like my man, but he's not like Sammy, he has a proper job, and he doesn't drink either."

As Megan listened she thought to herself, 'Well none of you have much to show for yourselves.' Nor did she think much of her aunt for not visiting her own father and not even coming to his funeral. Could it be all because of religion? Megan wondered, her husband being Prod and she being Fenian? If so, how awful!

Realising she had nothing in common with any of her relatives here in Belfast, Megan stood up and said, "I better get back now, my mistress will want to start lunch any minute now."

"Oh, you're all posh," her aunt said, "with yer lunch, now you're living on Malone Road."

"I'm glad you think so," Megan replied as she closed the door behind her.

Are you socially graced enough to socialise
As not to be embarrassed?

"Is everything alright, Megan?" Mrs Willis asked as they prepared lunch. "Will you be visiting your aunt now, sometime?"

"No indeed I won't, why should I want to know them? I could have been out on the street if it wasn't for Helen. Besides, you forget, Mrs Willis, I am a Fenian. I don't suppose her husband would have anything to do with me."

"Well, isn't she one of those – whatever you call them?"

"I'm not sure if she is a Catholic any more, living on the Shankhill Road. She's probably not told her neighbours either, but there again, she does talk like Brigit, so they'll know she's from the Irish Free State."

"My goodness, those people and their religion!" Mrs Willis

said, "We are all God's children, and He has no favourites."

As she said this Megan was thinking, 'I bet He has no skivvies in Heaven either,' but aloud she said, "Quite right you are, I've never known anything like this until I came to Belfast. All this stuff about Prods, Fenians, Peelers walking up and down dressed in black with big black boots and helmets, carrying guns, it's frightened the life out of me."

"Are you sure about all this Megan?" Mrs Willis asked.

"Sure about what?"

"This business about – what do you say – you know, these people you are calling Prods and Fenians and whatever else you call them."

"Yes, Fenians, and the big men in black with guns, yes I am sure. You want to get the master to take you up there to Ardoyne, and you'll see them all day long, walking up and down. Us kids used to have to get off the path, so as to let them by."

"Yes, I might do that, Megan, get master to go for a run and see for ourselves."

"Mind you, Mrs Willis, don't get lost in Ardoyne, there are rows upon rows of houses, great big long streets, the Prods live at the top of the streets and the Catholics are all at the bottom half."

"Don't they live side by side of each other?"

"Course not," Megan said, and laughed."

"Megan, why do you say, 'the Irish Free State'?"

"Well, I never heard that name mentioned until those RUC B Specials hit me. I think I told you before about this. That was when they called me over, and asked me my name and address, and when I did so, they said the 'F' word, and said 'she's from the F.. Irish Free State'."

"Well, Megan," Mrs Willis said laughing, "so you are from the Irish Free State, and I'm from England and we both live in Belfast, and I'm very glad to have known you, Megan. And with a bit of duck and dive, you will survive, I'm sure of that."

When you get used to silks
It's hard to live with sacks.

Whenever Megan went into Belfast City, or wherever she would see some poor scruffy child, she would always make a point of smiling and saying 'Hello' (and she still does), because she knows too well the feeling of being isolated and lonely, of having nothing, and of being despised for who she was.

So when she got her month's money, two pounds ten shillings in an envelope, Mrs Willis would ask her what she intended doing with it. She would go on to tell Megan, "Make sure you do your shopping first, before you meet some beggars, because I'm sure them same beggars must think you have come from a rich family, when they see you with pound notes, and you being so young. They don't realise how you have worked for it, so remember what I tell you, Megan, hold onto your money!"

But Megan still couldn't pass by a beggar without putting a few pennies at least in his hand, remembering how she herself had felt when the Irish-speaking Sister from Bundorran would look as if she had a permanent bad smell under her nose when she went near a poor child. When Megan looks back, she often thinks how much more she might have learnt, if it had been a smile she had got from that nun, instead of that awful look, despite having had nothing to eat before going to school sometimes.

On Sundays that same Sister would go visiting the school children's houses, and be all sweetness and light; then on Monday she'd have that look again, maybe because she couldn't stomach the poverty she had seen the day before.

Mrs Willis would tell Megan she wished that her son Tim would spend more time on his medical studies and less on his music. She was concerned that he wouldn't qualify as a doctor, let alone a consultant surgeon, which she hoped he would be one day. He not only played the grand piano which took up the whole of one side of the drawing room, he would also sit for hours writing music of his own, especially when his parents were out. Indeed, Megan could very often hear him in the early hours of the morning, practising what he had written.

The piano was constantly covered with scattered sheet-music, and bore a hand-lettered notice saying DON'T TOUCH. Other Queen's University students would often come with musical instruments, especially at Christmas. Megan loved going to the Carol Service in Mr Willis' Church, this is something else she had never experienced before, and for days later she and Mrs Willis could be heard singing all over the house. Mrs Willis couldn't stop laughing when she heard Megan singing, 'No Hell, No Hell', instead of 'Noel, Noel'.

Megan had bad chilblains on her hands and feet that year, and Mrs Willis would tell her to make sure she dried her hands properly and gave her Snow Fire cream, but it didn't help her hands much, as they were so seldom out of water.

There were so many domestic servants and nursemaids on the Malone Road, all attending the Catholic church, and without anywhere to go on their half days off, that the priest gave them a room at the back of the church where they could meet on Thursdays for a cup of tea and a biscuit – that is, those who could afford it. It was there that Megan heard the girls talking about going to England or America, and thought she would do the same, now that she was sixteen and a half.

"What are you doing with those papers?" Mrs Willis asked, when she saw them spread out on the big kitchen table.

"I'm looking for jobs in England or America."

"What kind of jobs?"

"Anything that I think I can do."

"The master and I wondered when you would be leaving for England, but don't you think you should wait a while longer, at least until after Christmas? Maybe by then the war will be over."

"Well, it will take some time before I can go, even if I did get a job in England or America."

"What about Helen if you go to America? You won't see her, maybe for a long while."

"Or maybe never," Megan replied.

"Well, I wouldn't say never," Mrs Willis said.

"Oh, I would say never."

"Why do you say that?"

"Well, back home in the Free State, when anyone goes to America, they have a wake for them before they go, its called the American Wake."

"Why is it called that?"

"Because they can never afford to come back home again. But I won't be having a Wake, because I won't want to come back. Besides, I would have no one who would miss me."

"Well, what about us? Won't we miss you?"

"Would you?"

"Course we will, you silly girl! But I know what you mean, it's people with families."

"Yes, and a lot of people from the Free State go to America. I've never known anyone to come back again, but they do send some money home, now and again, and clothes, to those they have left behind."

"And did you know some of those that went to America?"

"Yes I have, and every year about February, us kids would be asked to go up onto the Moat and pick shamrock, so they would send it to America for St Patrick's Day. Us poor kids got so used to picking shamrock, that we knew who to take it to, and they would pay us."

"How much?" Mrs Willis asked.

"It depends, sometimes sixpence or a shilling, there were special little boxes you could buy to put the Shamrock into before posting it off to America. But there wouldn't be English Wakes. No, I've never heard of anyone, just going to England, having a wake. Anyhow, most people I knew that went to America had been sponsored by a relative that was already there and had sent them the fare. My own aunt, my father's sister is in America, and the family she left behind get clothes and dollars quite often, but she never came back herself. I supposed if she's sending money and clothes back home, she cannot afford to come back."

CHAPTER TEN

"Look," Megan said, "look what I've found," pushing the paper so as Mrs Willis could read it:

Young girl wanted 16-18 years for light duties,
9-5pm five days a week 35/- per week.
Live in Temple Chamber, Temple Avenue
Fleet Street, London EC4

"That's an old paper you are reading," Mrs Willis said.
"Well, can I phone anyway? Please, please, Mrs Willis!"
"Well, yes, but I'm not sure about you taking off for London and not telling anyone."
"Oh, please can I ring?"
"I'll ask master, he's in the study, maybe he will ring for you."
Mrs Willis was ages upstairs, at least it seemed ages. "No, the job has not gone, master asked a few questions for you. The gentleman in London is going to ring you back."
Once again Megan said a silent prayer, and every time the phone rang she jumped, until at last it was for her, from Fleet Street, London. "How soon can you come?" a Mr Lorraine asked.
"One month's time," Megan shouted back.
"Oh, it will take longer than that, by the time we get things sorted out," Mr Lorraine went on.
"But the job is mine sir?"
"Yes, it's yours, and we will be in touch again soon."
"I must write to Helen," Megan said as she put the phone down, "I'm off to England, I'm off to England!" she shouted.
"Megan, you will need a passport to get to England, because you are from the South," Mr Willis said. "Have you got your birth certificate?"
"No I haven't, I forgot to take it with me when I ran away from Brigit's."

"Well, you will have to ask her for it."

"I can't do that, you don't know what they're like. I don't want to go near them."

"Well don't worry, we will write to your home town for another one."

"Thank you Mr Willis." Megan went on to say that sometimes a Baptismal certificate would do. "I'll write and ask Leonard to get me one from our church."

"Also, Megan, I think you should go and see your brothers before you leave for England," Mr Willis went on to say, laughing, "in case you decide to go on to America and never come back – knowing you!"

"Yes, I think that is a good idea, I will go and see Leonard and James."

But before she got around to visiting Leonard and James, she received a short letter from James saying, 'Megan meet me at the train station Belfast, Monday, 7.30pm.'

"Where is he coming to?" Mr Willis asked.

"I have no idea, and it's too late now to tell him not to come."

"How old is he?" Mr Willis went on.

"He's two and a half years older than me, so that would make him nineteen years old. Oh, what am I going to do with him? Brigit wouldn't want him, besides he has an awful temper, he would kill that Sammy."

"Listen Megan, you cannot do anything about him now. Meet him and take him back home with you when you go to collect the certificate."

"Yes, that's a good idea, I'll do that."

Megan did go to meet James, and in some strange way she was looking forward to seeing him again. The train arrived and everyone got off, but no sign of James.

"Are you Megan?" a railwayman asked.

"Yes I am."

"Well, I have a message for you," he said. "Your brother James was taken off the train at the border by the RUC."

"Why?" she asked, "God! Is he all right?"

"I suppose he is," the man said, "They'll probably put him on the next train back over the border."

Two days later, Megan herself went over the border and home to see Leonard, and to find out what had happened to James. Apparently James had decided to take pot luck and come to Belfast to look for work, not knowing about what might happen to him, nor where he was going to stay. He knew nothing about Sammy and Brigit and all the children, and as for Prods and Fenians and Peelers, he wouldn't know any more than Megan did when Helen had first told her, "You don't know what you are coming to here in Belfast." However, James didn't get that far, because when the train was about to cross the border a crowd of RUC boarded it, pulled him off, beat him up and told him to get the next train back to where he belonged.

Someone found him wandering and distressed, and after he managed to tell them what had been done to him, took him to a Roman Catholic church, where the priest put him up for the night and paid his fare home next day. When Megan heard this, she told James, "God was on your side, and it must be true when they say that an orphan's prayer gets to Heaven quicker than a lark's singing." Knowing James as she did, Megan knew he would have prayed out loud in a situation like that.

Megan did get her Certificate, and returning to Belfast she herself was worried if she would be pulled off the train, but when she was questioned as to why she was going to Belfast, she said she was a domestic servant and was returning after a few days' holiday. She would have like to have said, 'well someone has to do the skivvying in Belfast,' but thought better of it, and now she would be soon out of it for good.

Megan had her last Christmas with the Willises, but it took another eight months before she could get away. At times she thought she would lose the job in London, but promised herself, even if she did, come what might, she was going to England, once she got this passport. If not to London, then it would be to Helen in Bedford.

The war ended just before she left for London, and there were great celebrations everywhere. She wondered if this was the reason she hadn't received her passport, which was now long overdue. Meanwhile there were a lot of phone calls to and from London, enquiring why she still hadn't been able to give them a date, so that they could send her a ticket.

"I hear you're off to London," Professor Flynn said, as he stopped outside his house to talk to Megan.

"Yes I am."

With a laugh he replied, "Well, we won't be having a wake for you, seeing it's not America you're going to."

"Fancy you remembering that story – I mean about people going to America."

"Oh, I remember everything you tell me, Megan, indeed I do. But not everybody who leaves Ireland never returns," Professor Flynn said.

"Oh well, where I come from they don't come back. Besides, me – myself that is – if I went to America I wouldn't want to come back, not even from England would I come back, not to Belfast anyway. Maybe, one day when I am well off, I will come back to kiss the cross they hung me on.

"Well, my dear," Professor Flynn said, pushing a five pound note into her hand, "I'm sure whatever you do, you will do well. But wherever you go, take care, won't you? And may God go with you."

Professor Flynn never did mention Errol being a film star, nor did Megan ever see Errol Flynn, but Mrs Willis did, when he came riding up Cadogan Park on a horse. She also saw him from the top window of her house in his parents' garden, and said that in the flesh he was even more handsome than he was on film.

"You ought to find out what's happened to your passport," Mr Willis said, "would you like me to ring up for you?"

"Would you, please? I would be grateful."

Megan screamed when Mr Willis told her that her passport had been sent to the address in Ardoyne.

"But why? How did they know where you used to live?"

"I had to put on the form the address I came to, and why."

"You'll have to go and get it," Mr Willis told her.

"Oh no, you don't know them like I do!"

"But they cannot hold onto it, it's your property."

"God, I hate having to go up there!"

"Look, Megan, things are different now, they can't touch you. You have our phone number, if you need help. Now go."

Go she did, and as she got off the tram at Flax Street for the long haul up to Ardoyne, all the depressions of her time there came flooding back. She looked at the long entries behind the long rows of houses, still full of rubbish. When at last she got there, she was greeted by Mrs Brennan the next door neighbour, who was standing at her door. "Hello, wee Megan. God! I hardly recognise you, wee girl, you look great."

"Thank you, how are you?"

"Oh, still the same. You're not coming back here are ye?"

"No, indeed I'm not." Megan thought she had better keep her voice down as she said that. "I'm off to England soon, I've come to collect my passport, it was sent here by mistake."

"Oh God love ye, I hope you'll be alright. Brigit's out," Mrs Brennan said, "but he's there." (Meaning Sammy.) "Do you want to come in and wait?"

"What do you think I should do? I don't want to get you into trouble."

"Oh, don't worry about me, I still don't have anything to do with them. Come on, come in. Sit yerself down, lovely to see you again. God! I wondered whatever happened to you, we all thought you had gone back to the Free State, one of the kids said you had."

"Look, Mrs Brennan, I'm sorry I didn't tell you, but you see I took off in a hurry. I can't go into detail now, but I may need your help, I'm frightened."

"Anything, anything I will do for you."

"No doubt you will hear them shout, so will you listen? Any trouble, will you go to the phone box in Alliance Avenue – is it still there?"

"Don't you worry, wee Megan, I'll do better than that, you go in and I'll wait here."

Sammy was sitting in his usual place, still with a fag hanging out of his mouth. "What do you want?" he greeted her, "Go on, clear off, and talk to that aul Fenian, sticking her nose in where she's not wanted."

"I have come for my passport, look I see it on the mantelpiece."

"Ya, it's on the mantelpiece alright, but yer not having it."

"You can't keep it, it's mine."

"Can't we? You'll see if we can't!"

Megan could see Mrs Brennan going down the path and as she did so she shouted back at her mother, who was a widow and who lived with them, "I'll be back in half an hour, ma."

Good, Megan thought, she has gone to phone for help.

Brigit returned before any help came, and the shouting and bad language went on and on. "You are not going to England," Brigit shouted, "You are not eighteen." Brigit continued, "If it wasn't for me and Sammy bringing yer to Belfast, you'd still be in the workhouse."

Grabbing her shawl yet again, Brigit caught hold of Megan. "Come on, come on, come with me!" And she began taking Megan down to Crumlin Road Police Station, where the passport had come from. As Megan waited with Brigit, she wondered if the RUC would do the same to her as they had to James.

"Can I help you?" the sergeant said, with a look Megan thought he reserved specially for Fenians.

"Yes," Brigit said, and went on to tell him all about Megan, in the Irish Free State accent that the RUC love to hate.

Laying his pen down and leaning back to take a better look at them both, he said, "So you are off to England, wee girl?"

"Yes sir."

"To, London, I believe."

"Yes sir, it is."

"She thinks she is," Brigit said butting in and grinning as she looked at Megan's worried face.

Pushing his chair back and standing up, the sergeant came forward with his hand extended. "Well, good luck, Megan – 'tis Megan, isn't it?"

"Yes sir."

Then he went back to his desk, and picking up a sheet of paper he said, looking at Brigit, "As for you, give me that passport. It don't belong to you, it belongs to this wee girl."

"I've left it at home."

"Well, you must go back and get it." Then, taking in Brigit's pregnancy he said, "Go back with her, Megan, and collect it." Turning to Brigit he added, "And should you or that man of yours lay a finger on her I'll have you both arrested. I have enough information on you two, how you treated this wee girl, to get you into serious trouble – plus not reporting her missing at thirteen and a half, when she ran away." Shaking Megan's hand he wished her good luck and a safe journey.

On the long haul back up Flax Street, with the spinning mills to either side, Brigit kept up a continuous stream of grunted abuse and complaint, about how she was the eldest of them all and their mother had made her do everything in the house while she sewed; and how that was why she never got to school.

"Well, I couldn't help that," Megan replied. "You're very bitter, Brigit, and you're taking it out on me."

"Why shouldn't you do for me what I had to do for you and the rest of you?" Brigit exclaimed.

"Well that wasn't my fault, Brigit, and you didn't learn from it did you? Look at all the children you're having. And what about Peter?" Grabbing Megan by the scruff of the neck, she shouted, "And what about Peter? Who told you about Peter? He's adopted, yes, adopted!"

"No, Brigit, he's not adopted, he's yours well and truly."

Slapping Megan across the face, she snarled, "Smart alec, you think you know it all now you're living up on Malone Road. Look at you, you even talk different, you were never like the rest of us!"

Straightening herself from the blow, Megan said, "Yes,

Brigit, I'm glad you've noticed I am different. I always thought I was different, and let me tell you, Brigit, I won't be having a child every year, even after I get married. I want to get on, and when I do have children I want to give them all the things I didn't have. I'll make sure of that. I won't end up like you, all bitter and twisted about our mother, whom I've never known. And if you think I am going to slap you back you will wait a long time. I've moved on, Brigit, not down, and you cannot stand it, because for you there is no escape. But for me, please God, I will soon be out of Belfast for good and I don't even wish you any harm, I feel sorry for you and of course I will always pray for you."

Sammy was grinning from ear to ear when they got back, which did not prevent him from adding his own contribution to the shouting and abuse. "Shut up, shut up!" Brigit shouted back at him, "It's all your bloody fault." Then she went on to tell him what had happened at the police station.

"I knew that one next door would have something to do with it," was all Sammy replied.

At that point Mrs Brennan came to the door. "Yer right, I did. Ye two had it coming to you."

The Wheels of God's Machinery
Turn slowly but surely.

"Here you are, wee Megan," Mrs Brennan said, "here's a wee present for you." And she handed her a pair of nylons she had been sent by relatives in the South. However sorry Megan felt for Brigit as she looked at her, she couldn't help thinking she was partly to blame for the mess she was in. Did she need to have all those children, however lovely they were? And indeed the children were lovely, but God what a life! And what a future, with Sammy as their prime example.

"Do you want some tea?" Brigit asked Megan as she handed Sammy his mug.

"No, thank you," she said, glancing round the room she remembered cleaning so many times, with its lino-covered floor, cheap leatherette three-piece, its sideboard, and on the mantel piece two black figures and a clock. "I'll have to go now," she said, and with a last glance at Brigit, closed the door behind her.

"Bye, wee Megan," Mrs Brennan shouted after her as she walked down the path.

"Bye, Mrs Brennan and thanks for the nylons."

Then she walked for the last time down that depressing Flax Street, which she had walked so many times to pick up the rations from Liptons on Crumlin Road, and to school. As the tram took her along the Crumlin Road she took one last look at the Jail, the Mater Hospital, the Sister of Mercy Convent and St Patrick's Cathedral, where she had been confirmed. They brought all her old depressions flooding back.

> *Everybody has one person*
> *Buried in their heart*
> *Whom they find it hard to forgive.*

When Megan reached Cadogan Park she was both sad and joyous.

"Everything's alright, isn't it? Mrs Willis asked.

"Yes, yes it's just going back there and seeing all those places again. It brought back a lot of bad memories."

"Well, you've done it now, it's over. Come into the drawing room, master is in there and we'll all have a nice cup of tea."

Megan didn't usually have her afternoon tea in the drawing room with the family, so she went on to tell them about the police sergeant, and of course Mrs Brennan.

"Was that the lady who rang me?" Mr Willis asked.

"Yes it must be, but wasn't it her who told the police?" Megan asked.

"Well maybe, but I also spoke to them, we were worried about you," Mr Willis said. They went on to tell Megan that they were pleased that she was making an effort to better herself, and she was going to see Helen again, but at the same time they were sorry to be losing her, and would miss her, and of course miss her stories. But it wouldn't be fair to hold her back.

"I must write to Helen straight away, and tell her when I'm coming, and of course Leonard will want to know when I'm leaving Belfast."

"Does Leonard know why you ran away from Ardoyne?"

"Yes, I did tell him when I went to see him. Helen had told him as well. Yes, she told him it would have been better to have let me go into Navan Convent."

"And would it?"

"Well, not now, 'cos I might still be there, and I wouldn't be going to England, and I wouldn't have met you two."

"My dear, what a price to have paid to meet us! But we're glad you did, and we're glad to have known you. Did you say your sister's pregnant again?"

"Yes she is."

"Did she always wear a shawl?"

"Yes, and she wanted me to wear her shawl and carry the baby in it. Once when it was crying, she wanted me to walk up and down outside."

"And did you?"

"No, I put up a fight, and then she hit me, and asked me who the hell did I think I was. Back home in the Free State the older woman wear black shawls, it's only the gypsies who would come into town on a Fair Day who you would see wearing plaid shawls."

"What else did they have you doing?"

"Oh, lots of things. I can't remember, nor do I want to."

"Megan, it's good to talk about those things," Mr Willis said, "to get it out of your system. What about this business about you selling firewood, Mrs Willis was telling me about it?"

"Oh that, yes, she would send me to buy orange boxes, lots of them, for about sixpence each. Then we, that's Brigit and me, but mostly me, would break them up and tie them into small bundles. Then she would put them into an old pram and then send me out to sell them, I used to call on houses where there were children who went to the same school as me."

"Did they say anything to you, about it?"

"No, not really, they didn't talk to me much, and I didn't have anything to say to them either, but they were alright."

"No wonder you didn't like Ardoyne, and indeed Belfast now, with all those bad memories. What did your brother Leonard think about all this, was he very annoyed?"

"He said, 'Listen, Megan, we might be poor now, but we had a mother and father that anyone would have been proud of, and were well respected in our little town. Our only fault was that we were orphaned.' And that's true, Mr Willis, we were well respected back home, even though we were poor. Also, that little house we lived in, and Leonard still lives in, was our own. My other grandparents, my father's parents, that is, owned it before that, and gave it to my father. We had some lovely things in it, until that Jew man, that I've told you about, took them – yes took them, almost."

"Well, Megan, it's no great crime to be poor."

"Oh, I know that, but please God I will move on. So far He has protected me, as Helen always said, He is always around us, and we must pray. I don't want to go on about Brigit, but look at her! She's still in that two-bedroom house, God only knows where they all sleep, it was bad enough when I was there."

"So you think you have learned from what has happened to you Megan?"

"Indeed I have, and in a way I've been very lucky. It has made me stronger, and not to expect anything for nothing."

"Well, you go on thinking like that, Megan, and you'll do better."

She replied, with a laugh, "Look at me, Mr Willis, I've still got my feet on the ground, but now I have shoes on them."

Megan went into Belfast next day and bought a case with some of the money Professor Flynn had given her. She also had her hair cut, and on the following Thursday she left for London. As she waited for the train that would take her to Larne, where she would get the boat to Stranraer in Scotland, she was very nervous. All sorts of dire imaginings entered her head, so that when at last she got on that boat she stood on the top deck looking towards Belfast for the last time and said within herself, 'Dear Lord, you've given me the opportunity to do something with my life and I promise not to let you down.'

After the boat journey, she boarded the train from Stranraer to Kings Cross in London. It was an overnight journey and people seemed to be settling down for the night, but not Megan; she didn't want to miss anything, especially Kings Cross. The train chuffed and hissed out of the station, until at last it took off. As it travelled through the night, the wheels seemed to be saying, "Going home, going home." And, indeed, she was going home.

CHAPTER ELEVEN

When she arrived at Kings Cross Station, she followed the crowd and handed her ticket in. "Are you Megan?" a voice asked.

"Yes I am," she said smiling as never before.

"I'm Maria, from Temple Chambers."

"Oh, pleased to meet you, Maria," she replied, reaching out to shake Maria's hand.

Maria seemed to be a bit taken back, but still gave Megan a 'cold fish' handshake. Mr Willis had often impressed on Megan what a good firm handshake could tell you about a person, and though there proved to be nothing wrong with Maria, that handshake was rather off-putting.

"Did you have a good journey?"

"Yes, a great journey."

"You must be tired."

"No, not really."

"Come out this way, we'll get a cab."

By now Megan had gathered from her accent that Maria was from Belfast.

In the cab Maria said, "Mr Lorraine said you were from Belfast."

"Well yes, I have come from Belfast. But I originated from Southern Ireland."

"Yes, I thought you were from the Free State from your accent."

At that Megan's heart sank all the way to her feet. God! is history repeating itself?

"Did you go to school in Belfast?" Maria went on to ask.

"No I didn't, I went straight into service in Malone Road."

"H'm. Posh, Malone Road."

"Yes, it's very nice."

In between talking Megan was looking out of the cab window

at the buildings. Many were still boarded up from the bombing, but even so, London was beautiful to Megan.

Just before the cab turned off Fleet Street and into Bouverie Street Maria said, "Look, there's St Paul's."

"Oh yes, I did hear it was near to where I would be working and living. What do you do in Temple Chambers," Megan went on to ask.

"I'm the cook," she replied, and straight away Sally and the Belfast Docks flashed before Megan's eyes. 'My God, not again!' she thought. But never mind, I am in England now, and we will have to do as the English do, and if they are anything like Mr and Mrs Willis I will have nothing to worry about.

"Here we are now," Maria said, "Temple Chambers."

After settling with the cab-driver they went inside where they met a porter, who took them in the lift to the staff quarters on the top floor. There she met the other four girls, who welcomed her with open arms.

"You must be tired and hungry," Maria said again.

Never having had those words spoken to her before, Megan replied, "No, I'm alright." She noticed the girls all helping, one laying the table, another keeping an eye on the chip pan.

"It's fish and chips today, if that's okay with you?"

"Of course it is, can I be of any help?"

"Of course not, you've only just got here."

Not used to being waited on, Megan felt uncomfortable.

"There you are now," Maria said, "help yourself to bread and butter."

Another girl, called Betty, was pouring out the tea. By the time the meal was over, everybody knew everybody. Nina was from Australia, Peggy from London, as was Betty, from whom Megan would be taking over, and who was leaving to get married in September. "I'll show you your room," Maria said, "you might want to have a wee sleep." For once Megan didn't mind the characteristic Belfast 'wee girl' talk.

The room was big and comfortable, with three beds, a dressing table and wardrobes. "Betty and Peggy share this room with you, the bathroom and loo is next door. Now do you want to have a rest? I'll call you later."

"No, I'm fine."

"Well, come up when you've put your things away, get the lift right to the top floor. You will be alright, won't you? Or do you want me to wait for you?"

"Yes, I would rather you wait, Maria, if you wouldn't mind."

"No trouble, it's Friday now, we're all finished now until Monday, plenty of time, don't hurry."

"God! Have you nothing to do until Monday?"

"No, nothing, we do what we like. Usually we do our bits of washing, or cleaning our rooms etc., but we all help each other."

The girls went onto say that Maria was in charge of the food etc., otherwise they all mucked in and helped out with everything else. Indeed, it was like a family, the family that Megan longed for. "Can I do anything to help?" she asked as she watched the girls clear away.

"No, you just sit there, your turn will come soon enough."

"Does the Guv know Megan's here?" Peggy asked in her London accent.

"I don't think so, he wasn't in his office when we came in. Come on Megan, I'll see if Mr Lorraine's in his office, so as you can meet him before he goes off for the weekend."

The Guv, as Peggy called him, wasn't in his office, but there was a tall, good-looking woman sitting in his chair. "Hello, Miss Lorraine, is Mr Lorraine around?"

"No he's not, Maria, can I help?"

"Well, it's just to let him know that our new girl has just arrived. Megan, meet Miss Lorraine!"

"How do you do?" Megan said, reaching out to shake her hand, and noticing that Miss Lorraine seemed to be taken aback to find Megan was so well mannered.

"Oh, pleased to meet you too," she replied smiling. "You've just missed him, he won't be here now until Monday morning. But you can show Megan – it is Megan isn't it? – around, and where everything is."

"I've done that already," Maria replied.

"Well then, I hope you'll be very happy with us here in London, Megan, and I know the girls will look after you, and should you be worried about anything, please do not hesitate to come and see my father or me."

Shaking Miss Lorraine's hand once again, Megan said, "I know I will be happy here, and thank you once again."

"I'll leave a note to say I've seen Megan, and she can come and see Mr Lorraine on Monday."

"Thank you Miss Lorraine," Maria said, and closed the door. "That's Mr Lorraine's daughter, she pops in now and again. She works quite near here in a theatre."

"God, she's beautiful!" Megan said.

"That she is," Maria replied, probably thinking about how she herself looked: very plain, no nonsense, a bit like dear Mrs Willis, in fact. No glamour, no sparkle, hair just permed, then left to its own devices.

That Friday night, Megan finally went to bed after a lovely evening. Having said her silent prayers under the bedclothes, she suddenly found herself crying uncontrollably, for what she didn't know. Was it happiness, was it loneliness, or was it fear? She couldn't tell.

> *We are all prisoners of our past*
> *You can never escape from it*
> *However much we try.*

Next morning Megan was the first to wake, always having had, up until then, to be up at seven every morning. Although she had often thought to herself that it must be lovely to have a lie in, she was ready to get up. Even so, she decided to lie there so as not to disturb the other girls.

"Have you been awake long?" Peggy asked, "Did you sleep OK?"

"Yes I did sleep, thank you."

"Did Maria tell you last night that we don't have any special times for food on Saturdays or Sundays? Just go upstairs to staff quarters and help yourself to breakfast. Nina and me don't bother, but you may want some, so carry on and do as you want. Weekends we do as we like, if you know what I mean."

"So Maria won't want a hand upstairs?"

"Oh God no, there's nothing to do. Just relax, kid, when you go upstairs you'll find a big pile of papers if you want something to read. The night porter leaves them every morning before he goes off duty."

Maria was already up, so they sat and chatted over toast and marmalade. After breakfast Maria took her around the big building, showing her where and what she would be doing. "No doubt Mr Lorraine will show you again on Monday. Did you go out much in Belfast?" Maria asked.

"No, not really."

"You didn't go to any of the dances in Royal Avenue? You would have liked it there."

"So you must have been there, Maria."

"Yes, it was great fun, but we go to Hammersmith Palace every Saturday night, you'll like that."

"But I can't dance."

"Oh, you'll soon pick it up, the girls and I practise here, you'll soon learn. Do you like music?"

"Yes, I love it, and I love singing, by that I mean with other people."

"So you like a sing-song."

"Yes, any kind of music."

"I was going to say why don't you come with us tonight, but there again, Mr Lorraine might be angry, that we took you out before he has met you. So I won't go out myself tonight, I'll stay in with you."

"No don't do that, Maria, I'll be okay, as long as I've got something to do, or read, or can I do any vegetables for tomorrow?"

"No of course not! Yes, I will stay in tonight," Maria said again, "My chap will come here for the evening, he won't mind."

"So you've got a boyfriend?"

"I don't know so much about a boyfriend, I met him at the Pala, he's Irish, from the Free State."

Laughing, Megan said, "So he's a Fenian then."

"Yes he is. How did you know that?"

"Well, I got to know about those things living in Belfast. In Belfast they take it for granted that if you're from the Free State you're a Fenian."

"Are you a Fenian?" Maria asked.

"Yes I am, but it doesn't matter any more now that I'm here in London."

"No indeed."

"I don't suppose you would know where the Catholic church is around here?"

"Yes I do."

"Oh good."

"I'll tell you what, the girls and me usually go up Cheapside and Petticoat Lane Sunday mornings, that's a place where you can buy anything, as long as you've got money, even buy clothes without coupons. The Catholic church is along there."

"Thanks, Maria."

About midday Peggy and the others appeared in the staff room. "I'm still bloody knackered," Peggy said in her London accent, "I couldn't half kill a drink, my mouth's parched. Any tea in that pot?"

"I'll make you some," Megan said jumping up.

"Let her get it herself," Nina replied.

"Mind your own bleedin' business!" Peggy said, laughing, "I've done enough for you, many a time."

"Oh, I don't mind," Megan said, "I've been sitting down all morning, I need something to do."

"There you are, the kid says she needs something to do."

"You don't want to tell her that, she'll have you running after her."

"Shut up, you two, you'll put Megan off us before she really gets to know us."

"What are we having today, Maria, I mean for dinner?"

"I don't know yet, I haven't thought about it much."

Straight away, Megan thought of Mrs Willis and how organised she was. "Is it always like this on Saturdays – I mean, nothing to do?" Megan asked.

"Ya relax kid, you'll have bleedin' plenty to do all week, sit down, relax, relax," Peggy went on to say.

Megan did help Maria prepare the meal of steak and kidney pie plus rhubarb and custard or at least she did the veg whilst the other girls sat reading all the papers. After the meal was over they did the clearing up.

"You didn't eat much, Megan, don't you like steak and kidney pie?"

"Yes I do, but I'm still not very hungry, it must be the excitement of being here in London."

That was only one of the reasons, but the main reason was the pie itself; the pastry was soggy and the meat was hard. Again she remembered how when Mrs Willis made steak and kidney pie she would always cook the meat the day before. In fact steak and kidney pie was Megan's favourite.

After dinner Megan decided to write a few letters. "Have you got writing paper and stamps?" one of the girls asked.

"Yes I think so."

"Well if you haven't, don't ever buy any, we get all our writing paper and stamps from the reporters downstairs. Also, you can always find some in that cupboard over there. I haven't heard the lift bell go this afternoon, has anybody been asked to fetch the tea or coffee, or sandwiches for the reporters?"

"Maybe Jack got it for them."

"Yes, that's another thing, Megan. Very often on Saturdays we get asked by some of the reporters to fetch jugs of tea and coffee from the little cafe on the corner. If they want us they'll ring the lift bell, but you don't have to do it, if you don't want to, it's a favour we do for them. We don't mind because they're very nice."

"So you're not going to the Pala tonight, Maria?"

"No, not tonight."

"So will you be going to the Café De Paris? You usually go there nights when you don't go to the Pala."

"No I'm not going there either. Jim's coming round and tomorrow I'm taking Megan up Cheapside, Petticoat Lane. I want to show her where the church is."

"That's a good idea," Nina said, "and I'll cook the dinner tomorrow."

As she said that Megan saw Peggy giving Nina the thumbs up sign.

Megan wrote her letters on Saturday evening. Maria took her to Fleet Street to post them, and on the way back she asked Megan if she would like to have a look at St Paul's.

"Oh yes please, I'd love that." Once again Megan could not believe the kindness of those girls. Nothing was too much for them, and of course, Maria being a Prod from Belfast, Megan couldn't grasp why she was so helpful. Then she went on to remind herself that she was now in London, not Belfast, and she was free! Free! FREE! from all that nonsense for good.

She felt even more secure when she met Jim, Maria's boyfriend. Jim came from Cavan, and was Catholic and had a Free State accent and was courting a Protestant girl from Belfast. The likes of that could never happen in Belfast without trouble. After she had read all the Sunday papers on Saturday night, she decided to leave Jim and Maria alone and took herself off to bed. And although it was still early for her to be in bed, she slept soundly until six o'clock the next morning. Then she got dressed, moving around the room quietly so as not to wake the others. Upstairs she washed the cups left from the night before, and tidied the sitting room. From the top window she could see for miles across London, and yes, once again she could see ships and loads of sailors coming and going. She smiled to herself and thought, ships and water seem to follow me, I wonder if it's because I am a Cancer Sign, born on the 1st July.

About eight o'clock she made tea and took it down to the other girls, who asked her did she know it was Sunday morning and that they had never had tea served in bed before. Nina went on to tell Megan, "Relax, kid, you'll kill yourself, take it easy."

"Ya," Peggy the Londoner said, "you'll bleedin' wear yourself out."

"Oh, I can't sit and do nothing!"

"Make the best of it," they said, and went on to tell her, "You'll have plenty to do when you start work."

"What day is my bath day?" Megan asked.

"What you mean," Peggy said, "'What day?' You can have a bath whenever you like, every day if you want. Bleedin' hell, did you hear that Nina? 'What's her bath day?'"

"We heard you were living in a posh area in Belfast, and we can tell you were by your behaviour," Nina went on to say.

"Yes, I was living in a nice place, but I wasn't allowed to have a bath whenever I liked, only once a week, plus I had to have it in my own time, not in their time."

"So what did you do then?"

"Well, I got used to it, I just had good strip washes every night, and a bath once a week."

"Those bleedin' so-called posh people make me sick," Peggy said.

"Oh, they were nice people, some of them that is. Besides, they themselves only had one bath a week."

"Well now you know, me darlin', you can have as many baths here as you like, twice a day if you want, and if you want to get up at first bleedin' daylight," Peggy said, pulling the clothes over her head.

When Megan took the cups upstairs, Maria was up and reading the papers whilst she sipped her tea. "Did you have a good night?"

"Yes, thank you. I'd have brought you some tea, if I'd known where your room is."

"Good job you didn't, I can't stand tea in bed."

"Me neither," Megan said. "It's not that I ever had tea in bed, but I do like to get up and dressed as soon as I wake. I'm not used to staying in bed."

Megan thought she'd better get off the subject, before Sammy and Brigit came into the conversation. She wanted to forget all about Belfast, although now and again certain things would creep into her mind, bringing with them all the sadness and depression of the past. "After you and me have had something to eat," Maria said, "We'll go to Cheapside and Petticoat Lane and whatever, it's only walking distance from here."

Indeed the girls were right, you could buy anything in the way of clothes without coupons, so long as you had the money. Megan didn't buy much, apart from some underwear, as she was saving her bit of money for better things. "Look, there's your church," Maria said. "Do you want to go in? I'll wait here for you, I like browsing around here."

"No, I won't go today, but now I know where it is."

"Okay, are you sure about that?"

"Yes, yes, thank you Maria."

When they got back to Temple Chambers, Nina was waiting to dish up the meat, roast potatoes and greens, and afterwards they had peaches and custard. Again, Megan wanted to clear up, wash up, sweep up. Whatever sort of housework you care to mention, she wanted to do it.

"God! kid, relax! You make my nerves bad," Nina said.

"Ya, she's doin' my bleedin' head in," Peggy said.

"Oh I'm sorry," Megan said, "I don't mean to upset you, it's just that I'm not used to being waited on. I will try to relax."

"Yes, you do that," Peggy said. "If we want you to do anything, we'll ask you. Did you see anything down the Lane?"

"Yes, I did see a few things, but I'm not in a hurry for anything." She didn't want to say she thought a lot of it was rubbish, as she didn't want to offend anyone. Megan had other ideas about what clothes she would buy, once she could afford them. Moreover, she was saving such money as she had, because she wanted to visit Helen soon. She hadn't seen anything like Mrs Kennedy's Irish tweed coat, but one day, she had promised herself, she would have one like it, come what may.

At last Monday morning came. "Time to see the Guv," as Peggy called him. Maria took her down to his office, and after knocking on the door, she said to Megan, "Good luck, I'll see you later."

As he opened the door, Mr Lorraine walked past Megan, saying, "Take a seat, I'll be back shortly."

Whilst waiting she glanced round his office, and staring her in the face on the mantelpiece was a note in big, bold letters, which read, 'Your pretty, blue-eyed, fair-haired little girl has arrived.' When he returned, Megan stood up as he entered the room.

"Sit, sit girl."

"Thank you, sir." she said, although he was far from looking like a 'sir', or at least the ones she had met. He looked well into pensionable age, bent over and a bit miserable-looking. Maybe he's in pain, she thought. Megan was used to shaking hands with new people, and waited, but no handshake was proffered.

"So you are Megan. You're younger-looking than I imagined you would be, but never mind that for now. You're here now."

"Yes sir, I am."

"I suppose the girls have shown you around."

"Yes sir, they have."

"You may have been told, you will be seeing a lot of men in this building. You will have to watch yourself – you know what I mean, don't you?"

"Yes sir," she said, not really knowing what he meant.

He went on to read her the riot act, telling her that if she put one foot out of place, she would be on the next boat back to Belfast.

"Oh, you won't have any trouble from me, sir, I promise you that."

"No, somehow I don't think I will have any trouble with you, you look a nice type. But should you get any trouble from anyone, do not hesitate to come and see me."

"Yes sir, I will."

"You can go now."

"Thank you sir," she said as she leant forward to shake his hand, "it has been nice meeting you, Mr Lorraine, and thank you for the job."

Somewhat taken aback by her good manners, he stood up and opened the door for her, and as she added one final 'thank you, sir,' he replied, "Oh, Megan, one more thing."

"Yes sir?"

"Less of the 'sir'."

"Oh, right s.. ."

It was some time before Megan could slow down, as she still wanted to do everybody else's work as well as her own, which amounted to very little by her standards. Not only was this a doddle, everyone was so nice. She hardly got her hands wet, there was no serious cleaning, and no scrubbing. In fact she felt guilty at times taking the money, and wished she had more to do.

After a few months Megan had got to know London a bit better, at least well enough to get to St Pancras station and catch the Bedford train to visit Helen. Helen met her off the train in Bedford, and was delighted to see how well she looked, but Megan was taken aback at how sick and run-down Helen looked, although she said she was OK.

"What a difference," Helen said, "between meeting you now, and that awful day in Belfast."

"Oh God, Helen don't remind me! It's too depressing to think of it."

"Here we are," Helen said as she put the key in the door, "Look, Megan, all mine!"

"What do you mean, 'all mine'?"

"What I said, all mine."

"Why, have you bought it?"

"Well, I'm buying it."

The little two-up, two-down was spotless, with her utility furniture and home-made rugs scattered here and there.

"God, it's lovely, Helen – and it's all yours?"

"Yes, all mine."

"How are you able to be buying it?"

"Well, I've got Philip's army money, which isn't a great lot, and I'm working myself. And while I lived with Philip's parents it gave me the opportunity to save the few hundred pounds I needed to put down."

"Didn't you want to carry on living with his parents?"

"Well no, not really, even though they had plenty of room. I want a place of our own, for when Philip returns. It shouldn't be too long now before he's demobbed."

"Were his parents alright with you?"

"Well yes, but I had the feeling that they thought he could have done better for himself. Maybe it's because he's an only child and has been a bit spoilt, and now that they know I have a bad heart, they're worried that he's going to be left with an invalid. But I've got my little house now, and what I've got in it is paid for, so please God, when Philip comes home and he gets his job back, he'll take over – but enough about me, Megan. Now, tell me all about you and London, do you like it?"

"Oh I love it. But I tell you what, Helen, on the way to St Pancras I saw some notices in some windows which said 'Rooms to Let', and underneath it had 'No Blacks or Irish need apply'. Don't they like the Irish in London?"

"Oh, don't take any notice, Megan, those people probably had a bad experience and think we're all alike. Besides, you won't be needing any rooms, I hope, for a long while at least."

"No I won't, but I was thinking maybe ..."

"Oh I know what you're thinking, Megan, well you can forget it. There's no such thing as Prods and Fenians here in England, nor in London."

Megan had a lovely weekend with Helen, and was delighted how well she had done for herself. They talked about the past and their experiences well into the early hours of Saturday morning, then talked all through Saturday as well. Megan bought the fish and chips Saturday night, and on Sunday they went to 11 o'clock Mass. From there Helen took Megan to meet Philip's parents, they were perfectly courteous, but Megan did notice Philip's mother looking at Helen rather sidelong now and again, as she asked her how she had been, and when she had to go back to the doctor. "We hope you're looking after yourself," she concluded, and turning to Megan added, "Your sister's not well. She shouldn't be working and all that."

Helen told Megan when she got outside that what Philip's mother really meant by 'all that' was that she shouldn't be married in her state of health. Apparently she had already told Helen that. Helen went on to say, "I suppose in a way I can understand her fears for her son, but I really didn't know how bad I was until I came to England and went to a doctor. As you know I didn't go to a doctor in Belfast; in service you don't have to be sick, nor do you go to doctors."

Although Helen didn't want to take it, Megan did give her a pound note as she said goodbye at the Station, and went on helping her in that way every time she saw her after that. She would often put a ten shilling note in her letters to Leonard, as well.

When she arrived back very late on the Sunday night, the girls were very worried and asked where she had been.

"Oh, I got the last train into St Pancras. I went halfway down to get the underground, and as there was nobody around I got frightened and ran back, so I got a cab. "I think you had better stick to getting a cab, until you get to know London a bit better. Where were you going to get the underground train to?" Peggy asked.

"Well, like you said, to Charing Cross or Temple Bar, or Blackfriars."

"Well try not to go to Blackfriars, because it's very dark from there to here. I think you had better stick to getting a cab. Anyway, did you have a nice time?"

"Yes I did. It was nice seeing Helen again. Did you lot go to the Pala last night?" Megan asked.

"Course we did."

"Need I ask, did you have a nice time?"

"Tell Megan about the Yank, Peggy."

"Oh, you tell her, I can't. I'm too tired. I'm going to bed."

"What about the Yank?"

"Well, you know them beauty spots that Peggy puts on? Well

this Yank asked her to dance a second time, and in between she went to the loo. She noticed she'd lost her black spot, so she put another one on. So when the Yank asked her to dance again, he said, 'I swear to God you had that goddam beauty spot on the left hand side when I last danced with you.' She was so embarrassed about what he said, that when he said, 'Can I take you home?' she said, 'No, you're drunk'."

"And was he drunk?"

"Course not."

Looking at Nina and Betty, Megan said, "Did you two have a Yank?"

"No, not me," Betty said, "I'm waiting for my sailor."

"Oh, of course. I forgot you are engaged. How about you, Nina, did you have a Yank?"

"No, mine was an Australian."

"Are you seeing him again?"

"Maybe at the Café De Paris, on Thursday night. I told him I go there, he said he'll be there also. You'll have to come, Megan."

"Yes, I will when I get some more new clothes."

"Oh we can always lend you something. Go on! Come next Saturday night, you'll love it."

"Oh, I told Helen I would be coming down every weekend, she's on her own, and she's lonely."

"Yes, but what about you? You need to live as well."

"I'll see, maybe I'll come next Saturday. What's this Café De Paris like?"

"Oh, it's beautiful, but not as big as the Pala. All nationalities under the sun go there, you won't be allowed to sit down, plenty of dancing, you'll love it."

"But like I said, I don't dance."

"Oh just get up, you'll manage."

Megan didn't go to the Café De Paris on Thursday, but she did go to the Pala on Saturday. Wearing some of Nina's clothes and some of Betty's she felt like a fish out of water, and although she kept saying she couldn't dance, she wasn't allowed to sit down all night – nor, indeed, any night after that.

Christmas was coming now, and Betty had left. Megan had taken to buying more and more clothes off the Jewish stalls in the Lane, but still hadn't managed the lovely Irish tweed coat she had promised herself. Mrs Kennedy and Mrs Mercer had been very classy dressers, and Megan promised herself that one day she would dress like them. She coveted especially a double-breasted Irish tweed coat with patch pockets and a big collar. Mrs Kennedy would wear hers with real leather court shoes, handbag and gloves to match, and complete the outfit with a little beret, tilted to one side, with a brooch on the front. Megan would remind herself what Granddad would say: "Now there's class for you," he always said, "One can spot class, but you cannot describe it."

It was some time later, but Megan was determined to have this tweed coat and made up her mind that the next time she had to take the post up to the Strand post office, she would have a look to see what the fifty bob tailors had.

"Can I help you, madam?" The man asked.

"I don't know if you can, I haven't got a pattern, but I want a tweed coat made."

"That's no problem, madam, we have some patterns. You may find what you are looking for." He showed Megan a book, but there was nothing quite like her coat, so the gentlemen said, "Well, tell me and I'll write it down."

After she had told him what she wanted he said, "Would you like a costume of the same material, to go underneath it?"

"I hadn't thought of that, but I think it's a nice idea. I'm not sure if I'll have enough coupons, though."

After he had measured her, she said, "I'm up here every day at the post office so I'll call in tomorrow. Perhaps you will have the price ready, and I'll let you know about the coupons."

Holding the door open for this little five foot two inch urchin, he said, "I will look forward to seeing you tomorrow."

Megan did call back as promised, and handed over her clothes coupons plus a deposit of five pounds.

"You will have to come back a few times for fittings before they are finally ready. It will be between four and six weeks."

"Oh, that's OK, it will give me time to save the twenty pounds balance – you did say twenty five pounds, sir?"

"Yes, that's correct – for both that is, your costume and overcoat. Thank you again, and I'll see you in about two weeks' time for your first fitting."

I must stop going to the Pala so often, Megan said to herself, what with having to pay for cabs to and from Hammersmith, plus paying to go into the dance. And I mustn't forget Helen, yes poor Helen has come to rely on my pounds now and again, and of course Leonard, can't forget him either – and James.

Megan tried to be the one to get the reporters their tea, coffee and sandwiches, because the men would give her a couple of pound notes, telling her to keep the change. So on Saturdays she jumped up whenever the lift bell sounded – that is, if the other girls didn't want to go. They usually didn't, perhaps because they still had their hair in curlers, or indeed might still be in bed.

Megan did manage to get her shoes, but in brown suede, not in glace leather. She also got the bag and gloves, and of course her brown beret. When she showed them to the girls Peggy said, "Can't wait to see this bleedin' outfit, you won't want to know us and I fink we won't be good enough for ya – what ya fink, Nina?"

At last her suit and overcoat were ready, and on the way to pick them up she met Elkin Allen, a Jewish reporter from Temple Chambers. "Where are you off to?" he asked, and after she had told him the story, he said, "You'll be broke after this."

"Yes, it has been a long haul, but I've made it." She went on to tell him she was looking for extra work, as she felt she didn't have enough to do.

"Oh, you're not thinking of leaving us?"

"No I'm not, I love it where I am and everybody is so nice."

"So what is it you want to do?"

"I was thinking of an evening job, yes a few hours anytime after five thirty."

"Leave it with me," Mr Allen said, "I'll make enquiries when I go down the Strand. There's a nice restaurant called the Strand Brasserie."

The following Saturday, lo and behold, Mr Allen handed her a note, which said, 'Waitress needed in the Strand Brasserie, six until ten thirty, five shillings per week plus supper.' "It's only fifteen minutes down the road, you can walk there. I've told the Manager all about you."

"Gosh, thank you very much, Mr Allen."

"You're welcome. You must let me know how you get on, and I may see you in there sometime," he said.

Megan was now earning money faster than she could spend it. She would go to see Helen loaded up with gifts, and on Monday mornings Elkin Allen would ask how her weekend went. He laughed when she told him that whilst she was in the loo at St Pancras, a very finely dressed lady chatted her up, asking her where she worked, etc., etc. After Megan had told her all she wanted to know, the lady said, "Well that's not a lot of money for what you do in your two jobs. I could get you a better job than that, and a much nicer place to live. Think about it," she said, "and meet me here tomorrow night."

"And are you going to meet her?" Elkin Allen asked.

"No, because the girls upstairs say she's a madam."

"And do you know what a madam is?"

"I do now, but I didn't know until they told me."

"Were you taken in by this lady?"

"Yes, I suppose I was. I did tell her I would think about it."

"Well now you know, and don't ever talk to those sort of people again."

"Well she seemed a nice lady."

"Course she was, she's out to snare young runaways like you. That's where they hang out in railway stations."

Megan went on to tell him about another night when she got the late train to Blackfriars, and when she came out of the station a man in uniform asked her where she was going. Once she had told him he said, "Oh, I'm going that way. I'll walk with you."

After they had walked half the distance, he said, "Come up this way, it's a short cut."

Then, as if something or somebody had told her not to go, she bent down pulled her shoes off, and ran as fast as she could in her bare feet. It was so dark along by the Law Courts he wouldn't have seen where she went. When she got in the night porter said, "Good God, kid, what's up with you? You look frightened to death."

"I am," she said, standing there with her shoes in her hand and telling the porter what happened.

"There is no short cut where he was taking you," the porter said, "I've lived around here all of my life, and I know every nook and corner."

"God was looking after me then."

"He was indeed, Gal."

After that she never again used the underground at night.

When she told the girls upstairs, Peggy said, "He probably wasn't even a bleedin' copper."

Elkin Allen was also concerned when she told him, and warned her to be more careful. Elkin Allen was one of the nicest men in the building, and had given her tickets for various shows. Indeed, he asked Megan once if she had ever considered going to drama school, which of course she hadn't. Nor, indeed, had she known what it had meant. He had also mentioned to her something about him being on the radio under the name of Philips. Many years later Megan had a quick glance at Ready Steady Go, and noticed the name of Elkin Allen, but she will always remember Elkin Allen just as a nice gentlemen.

At Christmas there was great excitement, with all the girls talking about their Christmas envelope. "What's that?" Megan asked.

"Oh, Mr Lorraine puts a collection box in the lift for us, and all the men put something in. We usually get about fifteen pounds each in an envelope."

Megan nearly fainted at the thought of being given fifteen pounds all at once, and indeed she not only had the best

Christmas ever, but so did Helen, and of course Leonard and James. Megan will always be pleased that she helped Helen and that she spent Christmas with her.

"I got fifteen pounds, what did you get?" Peggy asked.

"Yes, I got the same," Megan said, "I can't believe it."

"I fink we deserve it," Peggy went on to say, "That bleedin' porter was grumbling about us getting the same as him, bleedin' cheek! He's a bit fick anyway."

Megan spent Christmas with Helen, although she knew she would be missing out on the fun in London. But Helen was lonely, and couldn't wait for Philip to be demobbed. Megan noticed Helen going downhill. She no longer felt able to go for a walk after Mass on Sundays, it took her all her time to get there and back. By now she had given up her job as a cleaner in a doctor's house; in fact the doctor told her he didn't think she was up to the job. And although Helen tried not to show it, Megan could see that her breathing was getting worse.

It was on one of those Sundays, when Helen and Megan were having their usual sing-song pretending they were on stage, and Helen was singing her favourite song 'If I were a Blackbird I'd whistle and sing, I'd follow my true love wherever he's been', when she had her first heart attack. She fell down and went all blue. Megan was petrified, especially as she didn't know anyone locally. She ran out of the back door to try to attract the neighbour whose window looked into Helen's garden. Megan said to herself once more, as she shouted for the neighbour, God, history really is repeating itself. When the next door neighbour came in, she said, "She really shouldn't be on her own, she's not at all well. We've been waiting for something like this to happen, my husband and me. Good job you're here."

Her husband had got on his bike and ridden off to get help, meanwhile the neighbour said, "She needs a drop of whisky to bring her round and we haven't got any."

"Where can I go to get some?"

"Well, you could try the pub on the corner, but it will be shut and whisky is scarce."

"Never mind," Megan said, "I'll go."

When she did get to the pub it was shut, and the back gate locked, but the barking of the dog brought the landlord out. Megan shouted as loud as she could, and in between crying, she told the man about Helen and that she needed a spoonful of whisky.

The man said, "Wait there." Then came out of the front door and ran up the street with Megan and the drop of whisky. Megan's still not sure if the whisky really brought Helen round, but she did come back to life. Even so, she had to be taken to hospital. "God, what am I going to do?" Megan said as she stood there crying. "I do have a job in London, in fact two jobs, I can't let them down, especially my main job because that's where I live."

"Look," the neighbour said, "there's nothing you can do here now. "If you give us your address, we will let you know, and the hospital will want to know who the next of kin is."

"Yes, yes, thank you, I'll give you the telephone number of where I am in London, if the Hospital should need it."

"Well, that would be handy for us as well."

Megan handed them one of the cards she had been given by Mr Lorraine in case she ever got lost, then asked, "Wouldn't it be right to let Helen's mother-in-law know what's happened? Then perhaps she could get in touch with Philip."

"Yes," the neighbour said, "I'll get my hubby to cycle down there. She'll be pleased from what Helen has told us about her. Now you go and we'll lock up. Helen has given us a key, she did this when she moved in, asking us to keep an eye on her. Poor girl, she's not at all well, and so looking forward to Philip being demobbed. You know how to get to the Station don't you?"

"Yes, just about, tell me again. Right, thank you and for your help and kindness to Helen."

"Oh, that's alright my dear, now you go and try not to worry." But before Megan left she added, "I'd better clear the table and wash up, you know, tidy up a bit. No, you go, me and me hubby will do that."

On the train back to St Pancras, Megan suddenly thought, God I never asked which hospital Helen was taken to. But then again, there couldn't be that many hospitals in Bedford, the operator would soon find the hospital number for her.

"You're back early," Maria said, "that spooky copper must have given you a fright."

"Can I use the phone please, Maria?"

"Course you can, kid, what's wrong?"

"Helen's had a heart attack, at her age!"

"What age is she?"

"She's twenty eight, but she had rheumatic fever when she was fifteen, and it's left her with a bad heart, but she didn't know that until she came to England, and she's been working hard to get her little home together for Philip returning."

"Poor little sod, what's going to happen now?" Peggy asked, "Will you have to look after her?"

"I don't know what's going to happen. Helen has a mother-in-law, but she's not very happy about Helen being sick, she's worried about her son Philip – Helen's husband that is. She had better things in mind for him."

"Have you got the number of the hospital?" Maria asked.

"No, Maria, I haven't, and I don't know which hospital she's in."

"Never mind, give me her name and I'll do it for you."

"Her name's Mrs Helen White."

"Here Megan, I've got the hospital. Here, talk to the Sister."

After Megan said who she was, the Sister said, "Yes she is very sick, but she's going to be alright. Her mother-in-law's here."

"Can I ring tomorrow?" Megan asked.

"Yes of course, ring anytime."

"Oh, one more thing," Megan said, "Will you take my name and address in London, also my telephone number, if you should need me?" Megan prayed hard that night, and until Helen came home again.

It was over a month before Helen could return to her own little house after she was discharged from hospital. During that time she went to live with Philip's mother, who never failed to remind her of her concern for Philip's future. Meanwhile, Megan cut her visiting time down to every second Saturday, returning to London the same day. She persevered with her two jobs, saving money even though she was still sending postal orders to Leonard.

"What's going to happen to me?" Helen asked Megan one Saturday, as they sat talking in the park. "I think Philip's mother would like me to go back home, and forget I ever met Philip."

"What would you like to do?" Megan asked, "Cos if you want to go back home I'll give you the money, and I'll send you some every week. I'm sure Leonard would love to have you back home."

"Oh Megan, I'm surprised at you talking like that, you know what we left behind! You yourself are always saying the only time you'd go back to Ireland would be to kiss the cross they hung you on."

"No, Helen, that was Belfast, not our little house in the South."

"But besides, Megan, I love Philip, and I'm sure he loves me whatever happens."

"Well, I suppose you know what you're doing."

All this was beginning to get to Megan. She would often ask herself what she herself had been put on this earth for. Was it just to look after other people? As the youngest of the family, she had already looked after and cared for, in one way or another, every other family member. But right now she felt she could not desert Helen; not now.

"How's your sister?" Elkin Allen asked on the Monday morning, "Is she better now?"

"Well, she's not quite better, she never will be quite right again, but she is up and about, at least that's something – isn't it?"

"You mustn't let it get to you, you're doing fine now, and you must look after yourself," he went on to tell her. "You can't take on the whole world."

"Well, that seems to be the story of my life."

"You're far too sensitive, it must be your birth sign, Cancer."

"How did you know that, Mr Allen?"

"Oh, a little bird told me."

That little bird was Maria, who was planning a bit of a party for Megan's eighteenth birthday.

"How's the waitress job going?" Elkin Allen went on to ask, "You still like it?"

"Oh, I love it."

"Is it hard?"

"Well, yes it is, you don't stop – or only for supper. But now I don't even stop for supper."

"Why not, don't you like the food?"

"Yes, yes, the food is wonderful..." but at that point she suddenly stopped and, being the quick-thinking person she was, said, "Well I am putting on too much weight."

"Course you aren't, my dear."

"Yes I am, I've got it well covered up, you can't see it."

She didn't want to tell him the real reason why she didn't have the food anymore. It was because of the rats. The staff at the restaurant including the many chefs, were quite as kind as the people in Temple Chambers. They called Megan 'Little Paddy', and she would laugh at this, as she had always laughed at whatever people had called her.

I learnt very early on to laugh at myself,
this helped me when others laughed at me.

She hadn't known about the rats until a particular night when she came through with a tray of empty dishes. The chef shouted, "Look out Little Paddy, duck Paddy, the big fellow's after you!" She laughed at this, thinking it was one of the men working in the kitchen that was after her. He had a reputation for trying to tickle the girls as they came through carrying trays.

Megan turned around to see nobody there. "Up above your head!" the chef shouted.

Looking up above the door, walking along on a ledge was a column of rats, rats as big as cats. After that she would shout before she came through the door, and was petrified every time in case one fell on her, but it wasn't so much that, that put her off the food, but what she saw when she was asked to come in one Saturday morning for a few hours.

As usual Megan was earlier than anyone else, and saw the chef lifting the many tea cloths that had been covering the trays of food left over from the night before, and cutting bits of meat off steaks and chops, and other meat, and throwing the bits in the bin. "Why are you doing that?" Megan asked the chef.

"Oh, the rats have been down here in the night, just wants tidying up a bit."

"God! have people been eating this?"

"Yes, so have you, didn't hurt you, did it now, nice bit of steak?"

Megan had to admit the steaks were nice, but never again did she eat anything there.

CHAPTER TWELVE

"I'm going back to my own little house soon," Helen told Megan.

"Oh good, you will be happier there won't you? But will you be okay?"

"Well, yes I hope so."

Then Megan's life was shattered at what Helen said next. "You'll come and live with me, Megan, it will be like old times, but better if you know what I mean." Helen went on, "I've got this little house and Philip's money and you could get a job, and give me board money. You can have the little back room to sleep in."

At the time Helen said this, Megan was not thinking straight, nor did she think what would happen when Philip was demobbed. It was only when she got back to London that it occurred to her that all this business about her moving to live with Helen could be Philip's mother's idea.

"I think you're bleeding mad," Peggy said.

Maria said, "Think about it, don't rush."

Nina said the same, and so did Elkin Allen. Megan thought about all the money she would be losing, the nice people she was working with, the money she was able to send to Leonard, and of course leaving Hammersmith Pala and the Cafe De Paris. But after many sleepless nights and worry, Helen won. Mr Lorraine said he would keep her job open for three months, but couldn't give her any longer, as the girls had offered to double up.

Lock, stock and barrel, Megan moved to live with Helen in Bedford. Helen was delighted and so was Philip's mother. She told Megan that her place was with her sister, who could not be left on her own. "Wait a while," Helen said, "before you get a job. You've got your Post Office book, haven't you?"

"Well yes, but I can't just do nothing. Besides my bit of money will soon go, remember I have to buy a bed for my room."

"Oh, Philip's mother is giving us one, and some bedding."

Little did Megan know, that this was the beginning of the end.

"There's an engineering works just over the bridge from here, the Igranic, about five minutes' walk, we will walk over there after Mass, so that you will know where to go on Monday."

"But I don't know anything about factory work."

"Oh, Edna next door works there, she does something on a machine, we'll ask her what she does."

When they spoke to Edna after Mass, she said, "Oh, there are plenty of jobs going there. Lots of people who worked there before the war are not all back yet, you'll be alright there, do you want me to ask for you?"

"No," Megan said, "thank you anyway," thinking she had done alright for herself so far, doing it her own way, "but perhaps you could get me an appointment?"

"Yes, I'll do that," Edna said.

The following Wednesday Megan dressed up in her tweed coat, shoes and bag, with her little beret on the side of her head, and off she went for a job in the Igranic. "I've got an appointment to see someone about a job."

"You must be Meg Glyn."

"Yes, that's right."

"What did you have in mind?" Mr French asked.

"Oh, I don't mind. As long as I can do it, anything."

"Yes? Anything, in the factory?" he went on to ask.

"Yes, in the factory," Megan said.

After asking a lot about herself, Mr French left the room, saying, "Please wait, I'll get someone else to talk to you."

A few minutes later another man came in. "I believe you want a job in the factory."

"Yes sir, or whatever."

"Would you not consider an office job?"

"Oh no," she said laughing, "the only thing I was any good at, at school was maths." Still laughing she went on to say, "and that was because the nun was kind to me. But everything else, no. I'd be too scared to do office work."

"Well, you can read and write," the man persisted.

"Just about," she said, still laughing.

"Well look," the man said, "we have a young lady whose young man was in the war, missing, presumed dead, but has been found alive in a Prisoner of War camp, and we have given her compassionate leave, so why don't you try her office job, until she's ready to return? By then we should know what suits you, but whatever, you won't be without a job."

"I'd be too frightened. Like I said, I've never done anything like that before."

"Look, my dear, it's all figures. Try it! I know you'll be fine."

"Your face!" Helen said, when she got back home.

"So would you be worried when I tell you what they've offered me."

"Worried?" Helen said, as she put one of her heart tablets in her mouth, "That's great, Megan. I'm not surprised they've offered you that job, they must have thought you were going to buy the place dressed up like that."

"Well, Helen, you know what Granddad used to tell us. If you are going into battle, dress up."

"No, I don't remember, Megan, it's you who would remember all those things. You're the only one of us who's like him. Anyway, I am very proud of you Megan, real proud, and so would Granddad be. We'll go to the pictures tonight, I'll treat you."

"No you won't, Helen, I'll treat you."

"Alright then, and I'll buy the fish and chips on our way home."

Megan took the office job, which paid two pounds five shillings a week, out of which she gave Helen one pound and five shillings. She did worry when she first started, but after a few weeks' training she was left to her own devices, and could do the job standing on her head. Again her boss would tell her to slow down. "The trouble with you, Megan, is you try too hard. You aren't giving that job a hundred percent, you're giving it a hundred and fifty percent."

"I know, but that's what I'm like."

"Oh, I'm not getting on to you, my dear, I'm just saying

spread it out a bit, otherwise you'll get fed up, not having enough to do."

Megan didn't feel she had enough to do, but stuck it out. Helen's health didn't seem too bad, and Megan missed London, for lots of things, including the money. She was taking money out of her Post Office book, but putting nothing back. The three months were now up, and she knew she would never get a job like London again.

During her stay with Helen, Megan learnt a few more things about members of her family whom she didn't know, and had never met, including another aunt in Belfast. "Where did she live?" Megan asked, "Why didn't I know about her before?"

"Oh, she died long before you were born, even I was too young to know her," Helen said, "but I used to hear our mother talk about her."

"Was that our mother's sister again?"

"Yes it was."

"Was she married?"

"Yes, she had two little boys, or so I believe."

"Did you meet those boys?"

"Yes, I did after their mother died, but I don't know where they are now."

"God! What happened to her?"

"The Black and Tans shot her on her own doorstep in the Falls Road, she was six months pregnant, it was a mistake they said."

"What's the Black and Tans, Helen?"

"Oh, I don't know much about them myself, I believe they were the British Army in the 1916-18 troubles, it wasn't talked about much at home."

"What happened to the little boys?"

"I don't really know, but they must be quite old now, with families of there own."

"God, Helen is all this true?"

"I don't know," she replied.

"So poor Granddad has had a bad time, one way or another."

"Yes indeed, Megan, but there again we all have, haven't we?

However, don't dwell on all this, it might be only hearsay."

"But we are out of it now, Helen."

"Yes," she replied, "and thank God too!"

"Yes, Helen, how about a song, can you manage it? You won't have another heart attack?"

"Good idea, Megan. Come on! The birds now are out of the cage and can afford to sing. Come on, let's sing!"

But Megan's evenings of singing were coming to an end. Philip was on his way home from Belgium. Helen was elated. Megan had never seen her so happy, and was delighted for her, but wished it had been a few months earlier so she could have gone back to London.

"You can stay here, Megan, when Philip comes back."

"Won't he mind?"

"Course not."

But Megan wondered about all sorts of things. What if Helen fell sick, what if they have a child – they will need the room, then. What if this, what if that! Also, what would he be like? Would he be like Sammy? No of course not, no one could be like him.

They plucked each other's eyebrows the night before Philip was due, and Helen tried on lots of Megan's clothes, as she herself hadn't been buying much, what with getting the home ready for Philip's return. Helen wore Megan's costume, belonging to the tweed three piece suit, while Megan wore the overcoat. Neither of them had any stockings, so they painted their legs with sun tan lotion, which almost froze stiff on them as they walked to the station.

With Philip's arrival, Megan thought Helen would have a heart attack, watching all those servicemen getting off the trains. "Look there he is, Philip, Philip!" she cried. He ran towards Helen, dropping all his heavy kit, and picking her up in his arms. Megan thought he would squeeze the life out of her, and she wouldn't be able to breathe.

Megan waited until it was all over before she introduced herself. She couldn't stop crying for Helen's happiness. Philip kept standing back to look at Helen, who indeed did look lovely, being as pronounced a brunette as Megan was fair.

"Hello Philip," Megan said, putting her hand out for him to shake.

"Oh, hello," he said.

Without realising it she had taken her hand back, and was feeling ashamed in case she embarrassed him.

Outside the Station they got a taxi, and in the taxi Helen and Philip had eyes only for each other. It was wonderful to see them so happy. Philip, of course, hadn't seen the little house before, and Helen was taking him by the hand, showing him the curtains she'd made, the cushions, and even the home-made rugs on the floor. She even took him out into the yard to show him the loo, with the newspapers cut into squares with a hole through them for the string to hang them on a nail.

Whilst all this was going on, Megan was laying the table, checking the oven where the shepherd's pie was cooking along with the rice pudding. "Where's the water jug Helen?" Megan asked.

"Oh, it's in the yard with the flowers in it. We should have had those on the table when Philip came in the door. Sorry I forgot your flowers Philip."

Megan didn't think Philip heard what Helen said as he followed her around the house, and she kept a low profile during dinner so as to let Helen and Philip talk.

After dinner they decided they must go and see Philip's parents, otherwise Helen would get into trouble. There was a social club at the Igranic, so Megan decided to go there to be out of their way. "You don't have to go out Megan," Helen said, "we won't be too long at Philip's parents, you can come if you like."

"No," Megan said, "I did say I might go to the club tonight, now Philip is here." She hadn't really, but thought she'd say this, so as not to hurt Helen.

Philip was there every day now, and when Megan got home, she felt uncomfortable with him around. She remained polite, even though his manners left something to be desired. Helen waited on him hand and foot, and Philip seemed to expect it. He was always served his meals first, and didn't wait for anyone else to start. Then he would ask for more, whether there was more or not. Helen would move some food off her plate to his, and he didn't refuse it.

As soon as he had finished eating he would roll a fag and light up, leaving his tin tobacco box and his fag papers on the table. Helen didn't seem to notice any of this, not even when he puffed the smoke across in her direction. Megan speculated that maybe his father did that, and Helen had got used to it whilst living with them, or maybe it was because she had never lived with Philip until now, and she was just getting to know him.

After about four weeks at home, Philip returned to his old job. Megan didn't really know what he did, or even which factory he worked in, but it couldn't be much of a job, as she had by now discovered that Philip wasn't very bright. On the other hand, as long as he was good to Helen, and didn't hit her as Sammy hit Brigit, Megan saw no cause to interfere. Helen had now made her bed, and she must lie in it.

Now Philip was back at work he came home at midday for his dinner, which Helen had on the table as soon as he walked through the door. Megan had whatever dinner she could afford in the canteen, so as not to put Helen to any trouble in the evening, even though Philip still expected something cooked again in the evenings. Even if it was just fish cakes and chips, it had to be something cooked. As his mother would say, "My Philip loves his grub, don't you boy?" He smiled at this, but couldn't answer because his mouth was so full.

"Do you fancy going to Cardington Camp tonight, Megan?" one of the girls at work suggested.

"What's Cardington Camp?"

"Oh, its a big RAF place, dancing every night."

"Why not?" she responded, being a bit fed up with things. Her savings were going, she had never got over London, and now there was Philip. "Yes, I'll come, how do you get there, Ann?"

"There's a special bus they put on for us. I'll call for you on my way to the pick-up point about seven."

"Thanks that would be really great."

Cardington Camp was packed that night, the dancing was great and Megan really enjoyed herself, she never sat down all night. After that it was Cardington Camp every opportunity Megan got. To her it was a life-saver.

"Well, what did you think?" Ann asked, "Will you be coming again?"

"Yes I will indeed, I love dancing."

"In that case come with us to the Corn Exchange Thursday night, it's lovely Glen Miller music there."

"What, Glen Miller?"

"No, just his records."

"Right, you're on. Anyway, I'll see you tomorrow."

"Goodnight."

"Yes, goodnight, Ann."

Then Philip suggested she should pay Helen a bit more money, as he reckoned twenty five shillings wasn't enough.

"I don't know what to say," Megan said, "I would give it to her if I had it. I really haven't enough left to buy my dinner at work."

"You're spending it on clothes."

"No I am not, that is my bit of savings to subsidise my wages."

When Megan got Helen on her own she said, "I'm sorry, Helen, I cannot give you any more money. Nearly all my Post Office money has gone, and I no longer send Leonard anything."

"Who said that to you about more money?"

"Philip did."

"Oh, don't take any notice of him, I don't know why he should say that to you – second thoughts it rings a bell now. His mother, that's what it would be, yes his mother. We were talking the other day, and she said something about all the clothes you had. I told her you had them before you came here."

"Please, Helen, don't say anything to Philip about it, I'd rather you didn't while I'm here. I am going to look at a bed-sit this weekend. One of the girls at the office has told me about a place."

"But you won't be able to feed yourself and pay for a room."

"Yes I will, the room is only seven and six a week."

"Oh, I feel awful about all this, Megan, after what you've given up to come here, I wish I could put the clock back."

Megan didn't answer that, for what she wanted to say would have hurt Helen, so she just told her, "Helen I am going to look at that room tonight, so I'll go straight from work."

"Yes, alright, Megan, but I don't feel very happy about it."

"About what, Helen?"

"You know, you moving out of here."

"Oh, don't you worry about me, you have a husband now to worry about, I'll be OK."

The room was so small, there was hardly enough room to turn around among the furniture, which was one small chest of drawers, a single bed and a small wardrobe.

"Where do I boil a kettle or cook anything?" Megan asked the landlady.

"Oh, you can use my kitchen. Come, I'll show you."

Again, the kitchen was so tiny, Megan wondered if this big fat lady ever got stuck in it.

"I don't suppose you'll be cooking much, if you're out all day."

"Well no, but I'll need to do something weekends, besides I can't afford to buy food in the canteen every day, and what about washing? – I mean a bath."

"Oh, I haven't got a bath," the landlady went on to say, "you'll have to use the public slipper baths, like I do. It only costs a shilling, and it's only a few streets away."

"Yes, I know where it is, my sister Helen and I go there."

"Well then, it's no big deal. So you will take the room then?"

"Can I think about it?" Megan asked, "you see I have another room to look at."

"Well, don't leave it too long, rooms are hard to get, especially cheap ones like this. We have a lot of Irish nurses looking for rooms."

"Yes, I'm sure you're right, I will let you know, say tomorrow, will that be OK?"

"Ya, I suppose so, but no later. Like I've said rooms, are hard to come by."

"Well, thank you again, I'll be in touch soon."

Megan did have another room to look at. It was much nicer, and she would have the use of a bath, but unfortunately it cost more than she was earning.

Megan wondered if she should go back to London and look for a room and a job there, but was put off by the memory of that sign – the one that read, 'Rooms to let' but 'No Blacks or Irish need apply'.

She therefore settled for the rabbit hutch and moved in a few days later. The room had no heating, it was damp, which was made worse with her trying to dry her wet clothes after she had washed them in the public baths on Friday night and carried them home in a old suitcase.

"What's up, kid?" her boss asked one morning. He had found her quite tearful, and was surprised as well as sympathetic. "Come on, that's not you, can't be that bad, can it now?"

Megan told him all about the grotty room, compared to what she had left in London. "I cannot see a way out!" she cried, "I can hardly afford the bus fare to work now I've moved from Helen's, I have to walk every morning, and I'm afraid I'll be late clocking in."

"Listen, Megan, I'll try and get you a bit more money. I'll go and see Mr Thompson, he's the man that decides the wages. It won't be enough for you to move, but perhaps enough for your bus fare."

Megan did get ten shillings a week extra, but was still struggling to feed herself, even though the boss's wife would put an extra sandwich in his lunch box for Megan every morning. Megan also sold some of her clothes to her landlady for her daughters, but she still wasn't getting enough to eat, and sometimes felt quite sick.

Then one day Megan noticed the tips of her fingers were

becoming swollen and very painful. She went to the doctor, who said she was very run down, and gave her some pills which made her better for a while, but those swollen fingertips recurred again and again, eventually becoming septic. Screaming with the pain from her fingertips, which had festering sores on both hands, she was sent to the hospital where a doctor lanced them, telling her that he had never seen anyone so run down as she was.

There was no unemployment or invalidity benefit in those days, so she had to sell more of her clothes to pay her rent. The doctor at the hospital had recommended her to drink some Guinness every day to build herself up, but apart from not being able to afford it she had never even been inside a pub, let alone to drinking Guinness there, so this advice was useless.

Then one day she met an airman from Cardington Camp, who asked her why she hadn't been to the dances lately. She told him she had been sick, and what the doctor had told her about the Guinness. Looking at her bandaged hands the airman, who was a drummer in the band, offered, "Come with me, I'll buy you a Guinness now."

Megan declined this offer, saying, "I've never been in a pub. Nice girls don't go in pubs."

"Well then wait here," he said. "I'll go and get you one."

She didn't like to hang about outside the pub, so she waited in a shop doorway a few yards away, and every week after that the airman would bring her a few bottles of Guinness which she kept in her room. She hated the taste of it, but it did help her to get better. Thus she was able to keep her office job and went back to the Cardington Camp dances, the Corn Exchange, and also the pictures with Ted, the drummer. After some eighteen months it seemed natural for them to get married, even though they had no proper place to live.

Her landlady told her she could stay in her room as long as she didn't get pregnant. Megan had no idea how easy it was to become pregnant; in fact neither of them did. With hindsight she can see very easily how wrong it was to get married so young and immature, especially without anywhere to set up home together, and ten and a half months after she was married, Megan had her little girl.

But before Patricia Ann was born, Megan knew she had to find somewhere else to live. She scoured the local papers, and haunted those newsagents and post offices which displayed cards with rooms and flats to let. But after walking, often for miles, to interview potential landladies, she was bluntly told, "Sorry, no children."

Then at last someone told her about a caravan site which had some caravans to let. The caravan was a small, single van that needed a lot doing to it, but she took it there and then. When Ted saw it, his face showed what he thought of it, but Megan shouted at him, "Well if you can get me anything better, then bloody well do it, because I'm tired walking miles chasing these places and doing a full time job."

By the time Patricia Ann was born everything was ready and paid for. Ted was demobbed and working by now, but even though Megan was making the best she could with what she had, he often fell into black moods. She attributed them to his regret at having taken on so much unwelcome responsibility, when he was still very young and not at all ready for it. He didn't complain, but he made his unhappiness apparent by his silences, rather than by saying anything, or even mentioning the subject

That was really worse for Megan to have to live with, and at times caused her great distress, which she could have very well done without. Considering the conditions that they were living in, she certainly made the best of the caravan and eventually it looked like a little palace. They added a lean-to, and even fenced off the plot, to make a garden for flowers and vegetables. But that backfired on them, as the landlord put the rent up.

"Or you can buy it," he said. "Two hundred pounds, take it or leave it. You know how hard it is to get places with children. I could let this tomorrow." And no doubt he could, thanks to all the work Megan had put into it.

Ted said, "Well, we'll just have to pay the extra rent."

"No we won't," Megan said, "We'll buy it."

"Oh, don't talk nonsense! Where are you going to find that sort of money on my wages of five pounds a week?"

"I'll get a job," she said, "Yes, a job in the evenings. When you come home you can look after Patricia."

Megan could tell by his face that he wasn't very pleased by this idea.

Next morning Megan was up early as usual, walked the three miles with the pram into town, and waited for the money-lender's office to open.

"I would like to borrow two to three hundred pounds," she said.

After he had taken all her particulars, including what she wanted the money for, the man said, "I'll have to come and see what you're buying. Next week then?"

"Right, next week."

"I'll see you then."

"Yes, thanks."

By the time the money-lender had come to see Megan she had found herself an evening job from 6.00 until 10.00pm at the railway station buffet bar making snacks, sandwiches etc., and washing up. On that basis she got her loan and bought the caravan, and there she stayed until Patricia was nearly four years old.

Then, when her son Eamonn was born, she sold the caravan and the family moved into a lovely flat, rented unfurnished. With the money from the sale of the caravan she furnished the whole flat, including a separate bedroom for Patricia.

From the flat they moved to a rented house, and when both children started school they (or really Megan, for Ted took no real part in the decision) decided to buy their own house. In fact the decision was much against Ted's instincts, and annoyed him greatly; his reaction was to tell her that if she wanted to get a rope around her neck, not to involve him.

Every day when she was picking the children up from school, after her school dinner job, she would admire the lovely houses that Wimpey were building on a nearby estate. She longed for one of them, and asked the site manager how much deposit one had to put down for one, assuming there were any plots left. After giving her all the necessary information he said, "Come and I'll show you around. Have you got a car?"

"Well no, not yet," she replied, "but maybe later, why do you ask?"

"Well, if you have a house without a garage it'll be cheaper."

"Oh, I want a garage as well," she said. Megan had no money at all when this conversation was taking place, but she dreamed big.

"So can I put your name down for this plot then?" the site manager asked.

"Oh yes," she said, "put my name on it."

"Oh, I should have said – your husband's name as well."

"Oh ... well I'm not so sure about that. You see, he's not very keen about getting a rope around his neck, Look, can you leave it with me for a week or so?"

"Yes, alright," the man said, "I'll tell you what I'll do. I'll provisionally book it, subject to confirmation after one week. Yes, one week."

"I'm by here every day, so I'll let you know, one way or another."

"Right, thanks."

The children were delighted they were going to have a new house with a garage.

"What house with a garage?" their dad asked at the dinner table.

"The house mum and us looked at today."

"Oh, eat your dinner and don't talk silly."

Megan could always tell by his face whether he was pleased or not, and nowadays it was nearly always not.

Next day on the way to the school she stopped to have another look at the building site. "You're soon back," the site manager said, "so I take it your old man isn't interested."

"Well, not exactly, but what I want to ask you is, assuming I did say yes, when do you think it will be ready?"

"Let me see," the man said, "Where are we now? February, yes February. I would say the latest June or early July, we should be out of here by then."

"Right," Megan said, "I'll aim for June then. Thanks again."

That night she sat down and worked out all her incomings and outgoings to see where she could cut back, so as to raise the deposit. By now they were enjoying a high standard of living compared to many she knew. They even had a TV and a fridge, which a lot of folk still didn't have in those days. This had been achieved partly because her husband had always been in work, but also in no small measure because of his handing over the money he made for Megan to manage.

Of course, she was still working herself, and as well as handling all the money she did a lot of home cooking and baking. Apart from this she made her own curtains and other household items, including some of the children's clothes.

"You've never had a bank account?" the bank manager said.

"No, I'm afraid not."

"Well, what makes you so sure you will be able to keep up the payments on this loan that you want as a deposit for this house?"

"Oh, I know I will. Look," she said, handing him the sheet of paper, with all her outgoings and incomings written on it.

"I see," he said looking at it. "You don't have much debt, I notice."

"No," she replied. "I try not to get into debt."

"Why hasn't your husband come with you?"

"He works out of town and it's late when he gets home."

"I see," he said looking over his spectacles long enough to make her feel uncomfortable. "Well," he continued, standing up. "When will this house be ready, did you say?"

"June, sir," she replied.

"Well," he concluded, "I've never done anything like this before – I mean for someone who doesn't even have an account with us – but I am going to give you the loan, and somehow I have a feeling you won't let me down."

"Oh no, sir, I won't do that."

"But," said the bank manager, "here take this and get your husband to sign it, then bring it back as soon as possible."

"Meanwhile," Megan said, "Can I book my plot officially now?"

Shaking her hand and opening the door for her, he said, "Yes, you can go ahead as soon as your husband signs this form."

Megan had told the children the day before what she had intended to do. "Are we having that house, mum?" Patricia asked before her dad came home.

"Yes we are," Megan said laughing.

"Did you hear that, Eamonn, mum said we are having that house!"

"What, the one with the garage?"

"Oh, we can put our four bikes in there."

"Yes," Megan said, "that is until we get a car."

"Are we having a car soon?"

"No, not soon, but we will have one."

"Dad will go mad," Patricia said, "when he hears about this house."

"Well, he's not going to know; not yet anyway."

"But you said he had to sign something, mum."

"Yes, I know."

"But won't he know then?"

"He won't sign it," Megan said, "You will be signing it, Patricia. Yes, you will put his name on it."

Megan disliked having to burden the children, especially Pat, with so much responsibility, so she asked them not to mention the house. But she knew that, whatever went on between herself and their father (and there were some terrible rows), they loved him. He loved them no less, and indeed as a breadwinner no one could fault him. Most of the rows were caused by lack of communication, for he would never want to talk about a problem, perhaps because he felt diminished if he was unable to present a cut-and-dried solution.

It was because he was unable to handle things, that Megan felt that she always had to assume control, make all the decisions, and shoulder the responsibility for them. Then, if she had made a wrong move, he would say, "I would never have done that."

Those words were always the opening signal for a big row, with Megan shouting back, "No, you don't make mistakes, because you don't make any bloody decisions."

This time Megan said to him, "We are having that house," but she waited until they were in bed, as she knew he wouldn't start a row whilst the children were asleep. "Did you hear what I said?" she went on, "We are having that house."

"Oh go to sleep, woman, don't bother me. If you want to get a rope around your neck, go ahead, but don't involve me, I'm going to sleep."

For the next six months. Megan cut back and 'made do and mended' even more than ever.

Megan and the children were now talking about the house openly. They would ride up on their bikes, to see how it was coming on, and were very excited every time an extra brick was added to the walls. A few weeks before the house was ready, Megan started putting things in boxes, and the children began packing their books and toys. But still Ted didn't mention the house, until one day their next-door neighbour, who had two very unruly children, greeted him as he came home from work with, "You miserable old sod!" It seemed that she resented his having told her son off (and quite rightly) for throwing stones at Eamonn.

"I shall be glad to get away from them brats next door," he said.

The children looked at Megan smiling from ear to ear, but without lifting her head up from the sewing machine, she said, "So you are coming then?"

"Well of course, you wouldn't be going without me, would you now?"

"Of course we would. With or without you, we are moving."

Of course that wasn't quite true, because she had included his wages when calculating the repayments. Moreover, she knew him well enough to be sure that once he had seen the house everything would be alright. It was just that had she waited for him to make the first move, she would have waited forever. Even when they were moving, he never asked who or where the cash was coming from, which may have been a compliment to Megan, but she would rather he shared the worries. But she knew if she showed any signs of worry over moving and the repayments she would be left where she was.

After the bank manager had given her a cheque book, and had put some money into the account for the deposit, he arranged the mortgage. By then Megan had left her school dinner job, but not before she got a clerical job with Post Office Telephones (which was later to become British Telecom). That increased her wages twofold, but added to her worries. As well as the worry of the move and the mortgage repayments, which were bad enough, she was stressed out by fears that she couldn't master the job. But she knew not to mention that at home, because his answer would be, "If you can't do the job, why take it on?"

They moved into their lovely house on the first of July, Megan's birthday. By now she had enough money for the legal fees, plus a few new items of furniture, to complete their new home. She even had a telephone installed as well.

But in fairness to Ted she could not have done it without her husband's wages, which he had never failed to give her. And indeed he worked very hard with the move, so that she could see he was pleased but wouldn't admit it. It was only several years later that he said, "This is the best thing we have ever done, buying this house." Megan forgave him the 'we', even though the decision had been entirely her own, made in the teeth of his sulky opposition.

CHAPTER THIRTEEN

That was all many years ago, now, and a lot of water has gone under the bridge. After Patricia and Eamonn left school, they both started working and paying board. Patricia became a legal secretary, with a car of her own; Eamonn is an Engineer working for British Telecom, and he also owns a car. Their father kept his own job with British Telecom and of course he also has a car, just as Megan had promised. She kept an eye on Patricia and Eamonn's finances even after they were fully adult. "Spend some, save some," she told them, and that is exactly what they did. Consequently, by the time they got married they each had enough to put down on houses of their own.

Patricia married Paul from Rainham, and has two children. Their son Grant has now graduated from the London School of Economics and works as an accountant for Fords, while their daughter Colette is an executive in a merchant bank in the City. They both still live at home, and are hoping to buy their own homes before moving away from their parents. Megan is very proud of Grant and Colette and gives full credit to Paul and Patricia. They are wonderful parents. Many thanks to you both.

Eamonn also married and had three children, Carl, Erica and Amanda. Sadly, Carl, who was eighteen years old and awaiting his exam results, was killed in his car on his way home from school. Carl had already mapped out a great future for himself, and is very sadly missed. Rest in Peace, Carl.

By the time Patricia and Eamonn got married, the financial pressure was well and truly lifted. Megan and Patricia would go shopping on Saturdays, while Eamonn and his Dad would go to the football. All this came to an end when the children left home, and it left a void in Megan's life. Patricia being very sensible, Megan could always talk to her about anything, and she felt she had a real friend in her daughter. Now, with them both gone, Megan could no longer see a purpose in her life. She had done what she had set out to do and was pleased with the results; though at times it had been tough, very tough. At times she wished for someone who would share her thoughts, her worries and of course her fears; she had thought many times in her life that it must be wonderful to have someone who would say, "Now tell me what is bothering you, tell me all about it, and we will sort it out."

She had admired people who had other people they could run to in a crisis, but that had never been the case with herself, in or out of marriage. It seemed that as well as crossing the bridges as she came to them, she had to drag every other bugger over as well! – just as her grandfather said her own mother had done. No one has ever said to Megan, "Step back, leave it to me."

All her life, for as long as she could remember, had been spent looking after other people, so she now decided she would see to herself, and try to find herself again. That, of course, meant freedom to do what she wanted to do without having to account to someone for every movement of every hour of every day. So she set out to find her real personality, yes, to find the real Megan, who talked to whom she liked, when she liked, and where she liked. You can only set out on such a quest alone.

After she left and got divorced she could have remarried, but having tasted the freedom of having a job and her own home, with all its comforts, and of course her many friends she turned marriage down. She has not regretted it, not one little bit. She feels better in health, mind, body and soul than she has ever been, and attributes this to less stress and aggravation. In other words Megan likes the new Megan she has found and so do other people.

They say it is better to be born lucky than rich. She believes she was born lucky, for despite what she has been through she knows how lucky she has been in having her two lovely children, who never brought her any trouble, and who are still two of her best friends. They were and still are very hard-working people, and would be a credit to any mother.

Patricia is a wonderful wife and mother herself, and of course Eamonn is also a son to be proud of and an excellent husband whose children adore him. Megan, of course, has many regrets, but her main regret is that she was so strict with her children. At the time she was too immature to think that maybe her children might turn against her, but she hopes now that they will understand that it was for their own sakes she worked, worked and took on yet more work.

The stress of it all made her bad-tempered, and she didn't realise how much pressure she put on the children, especially Patricia, who would be left lists of things to do during the school holidays, including looking after Eamonn. Recently Megan mentioned this to Patricia, who said, "Yes you were very strict but you were also a good mum." Megan hopes to be a good mum and grandmother for a long while yet, so her children and grandchildren will have fond memories of her. As the saying goes, 'One has to have nice memories, so that you have roses for Christmas.'

At the early stage in Megan's life, when she was leaving Belfast, she said, "At last, Dear Lord, I'm free and I trust you'll walk with me." She still believes He is walking with her, and she can now smell the roses, and the roses are all hers. The bird is out of the cage at last, and can now afford to sing.

Dear Lord you have given me so much, please give me two more things: a more grateful heart and peace of mind.

THE END

Note

Megan's sister Helen went on to have four children. She died shortly after the birth of her fourth child, aged thirty-eight. Each time she became pregnant her doctor would ask her did she want to go through with the pregnancy? Each time she would say, "Yes." She didn't believe in terminations.

Leonard went on to have four children.

At the last count Brigit's children numbered ten, and Leonard says she lived in the same house until she died.

James came to England in 1946. Megan looked him up after fifty years and discovered he also has ten children.